UПTHOLOGY 2

2011

UПTHANK BOOKS

First published in 2011
By Unthank Books
www.unthankbooks.com

Printed in England by Lightning Source, Milton Keynes

ISBN 978-0-9564223-6-1

Edited by Robin Jones and Ashley Stokes

Cover design by Ian Nettleton and Dan Nyman

CONTENTS
- UNTHOLOGY 2 -

Introduction

– The Editors –

In the Introduction to *Unthology No.1*, which we published a year ago, we explained that the aim of this *Unthology* series of short prose anthologies was to reverse a trend. We mentioned the lack of magazines featuring short stories; the uniform tone of the stories that are published; the inability of anyone other than a 'big name' to have their short stories published before their novel, and we touched on the suspicion that in the internet era readers themselves were losing the ability and interest to enjoy more lengthy, developed short stories.

It is heartening that since *Unthology 1*, although we've not witnessed a great upsurge in mass market enthusiasm for either collections or anthologies, we have detected plenty of green shoots and many rearguard actions among groups of writers, editors and readers who are not prepared to see the form wither just yet. *Unthology 1* found itself well-received by online journals like *The Short Review* and *Sabotage*, the former of which is doing as much as anyone to keep the discussion in circulation. Salt revived the old *Best British Short Story* annual, under the editorship of Nicholas Royle, and with it gave many of last year's stories a second wind. The BBC's National Short Story Award and accompanying Comma Press collection continued to generate press, as did first collections like Stuart Ever's *Ten Stories about Smoking*. The publication of Lydia Davis's *Collected Stories* proved a revelation to many readers who had not encountered her work before. Even so, in a landscape that is perhaps slightly less forbidding than is often assumed, *Unthology* still stands slightly apart in championing the format-buster, the novelette and the adventurous as well as the classic realist short story. We like to see stories rub up against one another like hassled commuters crammed into a train carriage. We like to see them fight for elbowroom.

The quality of writing presented to us this year has been inspiring and the quantity of it almost overwhelming. We continue to hold no restrictions on word count, content, theme or author-profile and humbly hope that this is encouraging to those who send us work and partly accounts for this deluge of excellent writing. Long may it continue.

The stories collected here come in many guises. Some are truly short, some not so. Some are really quite dark, focusing on the psychology of a warped individual or one of lives terribly afflicted. These may be leavened with humour but the world-view of the protagonist must be accepted first and stuck with if you are to be afforded the laughs. There is a huge diversity of styles, from the incredibly terse to the relatively ornate. There are mini-satires of contemporary habits or cliques, fugues on travel and places away from this tiny isle and there are alternative futures and parallel presents which are utterly recognisable but luckily still not yet the norm.

Possibly the main element provided by this selection is surprise. It might be the traditional shock of revelation right at the end of a piece or the jolt as you realise what is happening or who has narrated, but it might equally be amazement at the success of what at first seems quite an elaborate or bold enterprise, one initially uncomfortable to read or not as accessible as we are used to. We are sure that all of these stories deliver on the surprise factor, engender in us real thought, and enable us to look at the world with different eyes and with our balance readjusted.

Stuck

– Sarah Evans –

'Frigging snow,' Simon grumbled into his phone. 'And bastard airports,' he added for good measure. He waited, a finger plugging his ear to blunt the roar of chat and laughter from the bar. 'Sel?'

'Yes.' Selina's voice was as crisp as the snow falling outside the misted window into Wenceslas Square.

'Well it's hardly my fault I'm stuck here, now is it?' He sounded more defensive than he'd meant to. 'I can't help the fact it's snowing.'

'Not the snow itself, no.'

'Well then, what?'

'I can't talk to you when you're pissed.'

'I'm not pissed!' Immediately he noticed how the world was a little bleary. But he wasn't drunk. Not yet. 'You're not even here.' He could almost hear the soft *fuh* of her exasperation. 'What?' he repeated.

'I hardly need tell you, I always thought Prague was a mistake.'

But it was *his* bachelor party; he hardly needed to remind her of that and he wasn't going to.

'...this time of year...' Her voice jabbered on. '...weather so uncertain...supposed to be saving...' He held the phone a little away from his ear. '...mortgage...I managed perfectly well in London...'

3

He tried to remember why he had proposed. He pictured her long legs and shapely curves. They had wild sex. She could be stand-up comic funny, but could be sweet and tender too. They had fun. Or at least they had done till ten months ago when she'd turned moody on him. Finally, when he pressed her, she said she was tired of never knowing where they stood; she was nearly thirty now and she couldn't do the drinking, clubbing thing forever and if he meant it when he said he loved her then he'd do the decent thing.

Her little speech had sounded practised and yet slightly incoherent, as if she'd learnt her lines then fluffed them. *The decent thing.* Christ that sounded dismal! But she had looked so forlorn, her pale stillness such a contrast to her usual animation. 'Otherwise,' she said quietly, her eyes casting down to where her starburst nails picked at loose skin around her thumb. 'Maybe we should call it a day. If we don't want the same things. I'm not trying to nag you or anything. It's up to you.'

He took hold of her hand and his thumb stroked her palm.

'Course I love you,' he said, certain in that moment it was true. 'And I want to be with you...'

She looked up at him, her eyes wide and shining, and expectant.

And then he'd gone tripping onwards, following the logic: 'Selina, will you marry me?'

He thought, but only fleetingly, of going down on one knee. The corner of the table was in the way and the stone tiles of the Rose and Crown looked none too inviting. And besides he'd have looked a right eejit wouldn't he?

She continued looking at him, front teeth chewing on her lip, and he had the awful thought that she was about to erupt in a screech of laughter and all that stuff she'd said was just her way of dumping him.

'Please,' he said. 'I love you. Marry me.'

Then her face changed, abandoning her forlorn look so completely it was hard to believe it had ever been there. For a second she looked...but no, it was simply that she looked happy. She flung her arms around his neck and kissed him noisily with puckered lips. 'Yes,' she said, as she rubbed her lipstick from the corner of his mouth. 'Course I'll marry you.'

That look he'd glimpsed came back to him now. *Gleeful.* And the thought he'd pushed away at the time sprang up loud and clear: that he'd somehow been suckered into this.

'You'll miss the rehearsal,' she said.

'I'll just have to work on memorising my lines then.'

It was a joke. She must have known that, but she didn't laugh. From what he'd seen the vicar said the words in short, easy to remember sections to be recited back. Hardly taxing was it?

His eyes cast round the bar. Not like he'd organised a coachload. Just three friends, all of them mates since school. Bob had bailed out early, flying back today, riding out ahead of the approaching weather front. Tyler and Ryan were over by a pillar in the corner; they'd got chatting to a couple of women.

Selina was going on about all the last minute arrangements and checking up on things and how it would be her having to do *everything* now. 'So what's new?'

One of the women was blonde, the other dark.

Don't marry me then. He didn't actually say it.

The marriage thing might not have been so bad, over the last months he'd kept telling himself that. It was the palaver of picking a date and deciding on invitees and venue. Costing no small fortune too. And scented invitation cards and videographer and pretending to show an interest in wedding favours. Seating plans. The bouquet and the button holes. The three course menu and the champagne. Having to fight his corner: no way was he togging up in hat and tails. The umpteen tiers of wedding cake. The maid of honour and the bridesmaids and the best man and the ushers. He'd had to scotch the talk of pageboys too. The honeymoon.

'...and the dress adjustments still aren't right.' This last was delivered as a wail and he really didn't see how in any way that could be his fault.

The dress.

He hadn't been party, not directly, to any of the talk about that. But he couldn't help but overhear the conversations on the phone. *Bodice; corsetry; full, sleek, ballerina.* A whole new vocabulary seemed to be required. *Grecian column; Empire line.* A pile of magazines had sprouted by the sofa in Selina's bedsit, and she and her mum had spent a day – a whole sodding day – at a brides' fair. She came back both fired up and a little dejected, because although she'd seen and tried on so many heavenly gowns, she hadn't found *the one*, she knew that. But she would do, if she kept on looking. 'Just like I found you,' she said, her finger tapping the tip of his nose. He smiled back, though actually he was thinking that being compared to a dress wasn't exactly a great cop.

'You'll look fabulous whatever,' he said now and got another *fuh*-ed response. 'Main thing I'll be interested in is getting you out of it.'

Her spurt of laughter was followed by expressive silence. In the wrong. Again!

'Look, I'll be back soon as I can,' he said.

'Yeah. Sure.'

'Love you.'

'Love you too.' Her voice was muted. 'If only you hadn't had to fly somewhere.' Her told-you-so tone sounded like her mother; he'd been noticing that just recently.

He switched the phone off and breathed in the sour smell of beer and bodies. The one indisputably good thing about the getting married lark was having a bachelor party. Where did the word *unreasonable* feature in that?

Tyler had been to Budapest. Ryan had chosen Brussels and they'd all got so horribly sick on Kriek that he'd not been able to face a cherry since. So here they were in Prague and it was *not*, repeat *not*, his fault that there was so much bleeding snow and all flights tomorrow had been cancelled.

He pushed his way over towards where his mates formed half of a gesticulating quartet. The women were tall with sleek hair, glossy skin and tight clothes. The four of them were laughing. Flirting. So far there'd been none of that, not really. They'd done the strip-club thing but nothing more. The bleary memory of jangling tassels and gyrating suppleness left him somewhat dizzy.

Only as he approached did he notice a third woman. Her eyes gazed into the distance, her face tight and lips unsmiling. Tyler's arm captured him in a body-toppling hug. 'And this here's Simon,' Tyler said. 'Last bid for...' His voice was lost amidst the cacophony of the bar.

Tyler stank of sweat. His forehead dripped like the condensation on the bottle that he thrust into Simon's hand, like the sweat sliding down into the blonde's canyon of a cleavage. *Forsaking all others.* That was how the line went wasn't it? No other woman. *Ever.*

Somehow sex with Selina had mutated from a one-nighter of energetic, no-commitment pleasure, into *until death do us part*. The death bit was something of a turn off.

Except he hadn't made the rather dismal promise yet, now had he?

Except...

The pairings had already happened, he could see that from the sideways smiles and glances. Resentment flashed. This was *his* weekend. *He* was the bachelor. He slugged back from the bottle, the sharp fizz tickling down his throat to mingle with the resentment churning in his stomach.

His eyes turned to the third woman.

She was shorter than her companions, or was that just because she wasn't wearing skyscraper heels? Her hair fell more naturally: less styled, no highlights, less glisten. She wasn't wearing much in the way of make-up, and her blouse hung in pastel cotton folds, rather than clinging glitter-tight. But the main difference, he thought, was the sense of her detachment.

He shuffled over to be closer to her, catching Ryan's exaggerated wink as he did so.

'I'm Simon,' he said.

She nodded, but didn't reply.

'And you?'

'Katherine.' She conceded her rather laborious name reluctantly, as if even that was more than she wanted to part with.

'You're here for the weekend?'

She nodded again.

'Me too. Bachelor thing. We were due to fly back tomorrow. Looking dubious though.' Her look remained icy. 'How about you?'

'Our flight's supposed to be tomorrow too. Like you say, looking unlikely.'

'And what's the occasion?'

'Hen party.' Her face flushed. 'My cousin.' She nodded over at the blonde who was draping her arm around Tyler's neck. 'I'm only here because I'm a bridesmaid, and I'm only a bridesmaid because our mums are sisters. I hate this.'

'What, Prague?' he asked, his arm gesturing towards the window.

'Not Prague, no. The *not getting to see* Prague. The coming here purely for the drinking and the…' She shrugged derisively.

He gulped down the last of his beer, which was gassy and acidic. 'Speaking of which can I get you a drink?'

'No,' she said. 'Thank-you.'

'Sure?'

He felt weary. They'd already had two heavy drinking nights and now he was a good part through his third. His body didn't cope as easily as it would have a decade ago.

He looked over at the blonde woman and then the dark. Selina's hair was midway in shade between them and she was sexier than either. He wished suddenly she was here, wished that when he got back to the hotel room, he could just tumble into bed beside her and snuggle up to the yielding warmth of her body.

'I'm leaving,' Katherine said.

'Me too.' He decided it abruptly. There were spirits in his mini-bar and multi-channels on TV. He couldn't hang around here playing gooseberry. 'Where are you staying?'

Her look would have frozen the Red Sea. He laughed. 'I was only asking. I was only thinking that if we're headed in the same direction we could walk a bit of the way together. Stop us both getting lost in the snow.'

She hesitated before reeling off the name of a hotel and street.

'Not far from me,' he said. Since being here he'd drifted alongside the others and hadn't a clue where she meant. 'I'll walk you home. Just that. Promise! Scout's honour.' He raised his fingers to his forehead, realising he had no idea what scout's honour was and hoping his salute wasn't Nazi-like.

She smiled, and with her features softening he saw more fully how attractive she was with her high cheekbones, pale skin and unsettling eyes. The sort of face you might sculpt in stone. *Classy.* That had never been his type.

He offered back-thumping farewells to Tyler and Ryan. Ryan wolf-whistled; Tyler made a crude gesture. Simon tried to ignore them as he walked alongside Katherine to the door. He glanced at her set face. 'Sorry,' he said, jerking his thumb behind him. She pulled on a woollen Peruvian hat with bobble, which left her face looking almost teenage and vulnerable.

Outside, the cold sliced through him, instantly sobering. The snow crunched beneath his feet. Katherine stumbled forward, one slip-on shoe half stuck in the snow, and he reached out to steady her. She shied away and he put his hands up in self-defence. She stepped forward again and her foot slid. 'Stupid bloody shoes,' she said and he thought of her companions' stilettos.

'Here,' he said. 'I'm only offering a steady arm. Four legs better than two.'

She graced him with a smile and it felt like a major achievement.

'Sorry,' she said. 'All weekend we've been pursued by drunken, leering men. I've become paranoid.' She took his arm and he felt a jab of guilt at being excused from her description.

They proceeded slowly, traversing the long length of Wenceslas Square. Stalls were selling fried cheese and red sausages, and the stench of hot fat left him wavering between nausea and craving. 'Hardly a *square*,' he said, 'unless my geometry is very much amiss.' She allowed him another smile. Her body nudged against his as she slid sideways from time to time. The snow was still falling, but gently, and he stopped to shake it from his hair and watched her brush it from her hat.

She led the way along narrow roads, hemmed in by tall buildings. The road then opened out and he recognised the twin towers, all lit up, with their Disney-castle baubles, spikes and pinnacles, which meant they'd reached the Old Square. A rugby team of lads was headed for them, all wearing outlandish wigs and dressed – despite the weather – in orange T-shirts emblazoned with the name *Dave*. He pulled her into a doorway to let them pass and she cried 'Ugh' and turned her face into his shoulder, as one of the team erupted with a spray of vomit.

They started walking again. 'All people come here to do is drink and throw up,' she said. 'And the city's so beautiful, especially in the snow. Centuries of history.'

'History never was my strong point,' he said. Over the last two days, he'd of course had a sense of the antiquated surroundings, but he hadn't paused to distinguish the churches from the municipal buildings, the truly old from the less so.

'I don't know a lot either,' she said, her eyes down and her pale cheeks flushed from the cold. 'I did manage to sneak away for a walking tour and I have the guidebook I brought, but I don't feel I've got to see Prague.'

'I know that's famous,' he said and pointed at the elaborate, gold and blue clock with multiple dials.

'The astronomical clock. Made in 1410,' she reeled off. 'They had the clock maker blinded so he'd never be able to design another for someone else.'

He grimaced. 'Too much information.' And she laughed.

They continued into another maze of side-streets, then all too soon she raised her arm and pointed to a hotel whose beige-painted façade looked exactly like his own. 'This is it.'

His feet were numb. 'Your feet must be frozen,' he said, thinking of her flimsy shoes.

'Serves me right for not wearing boots.' She smiled and he felt the urge to kiss her, feeling it press all the stronger for knowing there wasn't a chance she'd let him.

'Well,' she said, her tone final and brokering no opening. 'Thanks for walking me back.'

'I don't suppose...' he started, and moved just a little closer. He had to at least try.

'No,' she said, stepping back.

'You haven't heard what I was going to propose.'

'I don't have to.'

'I was only thinking a nightcap in the bar. Give both of us the chance to warm up.'

She continued looking at him, her face giving no sign of relenting.

'Otherwise...' He hesitated, seeking something that she wouldn't instantly dismiss. 'Perhaps we could meet up tomorrow. Have a proper look round. Given we're both stuck here.'

She looked away, then back.

'Two tourists more fun than one,' he said. He waited for her to say *no*.

Finally, she simply shrugged. 'OK. Assuming there's no change in the weather. I'll be ready at ten.'

'Tomorrow at ten.' He was still smiling as he walked away, and the cold no longer seemed so biting. He thought of ringing Selina again, but it was late and he remembered her hectoring tone. And while he had done nothing – nothing at all – that he needed to hide, he was aware of not wanting to be pushed into the evasions which would keep his arrangement for tomorrow secret.

He woke after eight hours sleep, feeling blackbird alert and eager for the day. He listened to the airline's rolling message. Still no flights. At least no new arrivals meant he got to keep his hotel room. At breakfast, he ignored the stupidly wide array, sticking to what he knew: cornflakes, eggs, black coffee. He texted work. Tyler and Ryan failed to emerge. Good!

Outside, it was a champagne morning: cold, crisp and sparkling. It felt eerily quiet with the rumbles of roadworks absorbed into the layer of snow and only a dash of skidding traffic. Cotton wool packed around the buildings, smoothing out the sharp edges and rendering everything unsullied. His feet carved out new tracks. He'd left plenty of time, then found to his dismay that he'd taken a wrong turn. A small panic set up cartwheels in his stomach as he stumbled forward, half running, his white-mist breath hard and fast. It was ten past ten when he reached the hotel.

She wasn't there.

Shit!

His disappointment was acute. Their *arrangement* had been casual and she would have been half expecting him not to show, so when he wasn't there at ten precisely, she would simply have carried on.

He knew all this with certainty.

Perhaps she'd made an even earlier get away, had only said *yes* to be rid of him last night.

The day seemed bleak and empty on his own.

He paused, his feet scuffing the snow, not to wait, but because he couldn't think what to do. He looked down at the pattern of footsteps in the snow and wondered if he could make out which were hers, and whether he could follow her trail.

'Hi!'

He turned at the sound of a voice behind him. She stood there, all bundled up in that Peruvian hat, scarf and padded jacket, below which were black jeans and sturdy fur-trimmed boots. Her face was pale and pink and she looked surprised, he thought, but not displeased.

'Hi.' He tried to rein back his foolish grin.

'Sorry! I would have been on time. Raquel – my cousin – appeared at breakfast just as I'd finished and it seemed rude to dash off.'

'Was she…?'

'On her own? Yes actually. I'm not quite sure…well anyway. None of my business.'

'What did you tell her?'

'Just that I was going sightseeing.'

'Yes.'

'Which is what we're doing?'

'Yes, of course.'

'Any ideas?'

He looked back at her.

She smiled at him indulgently. 'Where to start?'

'You're the one with the guide book.'

'OK. I thought we could start with the Old Town Square.'

'OK.'

'I know we've both probably walked through it dozens of times, but even the tour guide seemed to whiz through it and I feel I've not stopped, not really, to look. I mean if that's alright.'

'That's fine.'

He offered her his arm.

She smiled and gestured at her feet. 'Boots! Much more sensible!'

'You still might slip. Or I might.'

She laughed, her white teeth glinting like the snow in sunlight, and she took firm hold.

They walked, her shoulder pressing snugly against his. They paused from time to time in front of pink and orange buildings while she offered commentary from her guidebook. *Gothic. Baroque. Romanesque.* The vocabulary was as alien as that of wedding dresses, but he tried to imbibe from her a sense of history and of awe.

They headed towards the door between the twin towers. Inside was just a church, like churches everywhere, but she showed him the tombstone of some astronomer who lost his nose in a duel, and they laughed at the account of his wardrobe of prosthetics – silver, gold or copper depending on the occasion. *Which best for a wedding?* He didn't say it. And then there was the tale of the guy's pet elk who died after drinking too much beer and falling down the stairs.

He sat on a shiny wooden pew while she went to find the toilets and he felt the solemnity press down on him as he breathed in the musty scent of tradition. The red brick church in Selina's hometown – its low ceiling and school-hall functionality – was nothing like this of course. Footsteps echoed, and closing his eyes he tried to conjure Selina's energetic steps coming down the aisle to meet him waiting at the front. Amidst the tourist murmurs, he imagined her voice, resonating outwards. 'I Selina Dayton take you Simon Matthews…'

Lawful. Wedded. Husband. It was hard to connect the words to himself. He remembered Ryan, his last minute get-me-out-of-here panic, and having to bolster him along. He thought of Ryan last night, his neck draped with that blonde. When he opened his eyes, there was Katherine padding towards him silently, her gaze still scanning the church, before it alighted on him and her face lit up in a smile.

They continued to walk the streets, mingling with the tourist groups and pairs of lovers, following in the snow-trails set by others. They stopped for coffee and later lunch, then coffee again. They climbed the hill to the heavily fortified castle and the cathedral with its stained glass windows and the tower with steps winding up endlessly towards the view of the red-roofed, icing-sugar-topped town. Everything seemed to pass in slow motion, as if the snow had altered time itself, not just dampened down the movements of the usually busy city. The conversation drifted from sightseeing into small disclosures and reminiscences. They had opposite tastes in films and books. They liked some of the same music. She listened to what he said quietly, thoughtfully, and he felt no need of his usual get-them-laughing buffoonery.

She worked in an opticians, she said, helping customers select their glasses. Working with people every day was different but she wanted eventually to train to be an optometrist herself.

'Insurance,' he offered back in his turn. 'On the phone all day. Gift of the gab.' He didn't add how each hour was identical to the last as he took potential clients through the exact same set of questions. *And does your property have a Chubb lock? And locks on every window?* And how he could not imagine doing anything different.

It was dark by the time they stood on Charles Bridge and gazed out over the lit-up line of the river, with the white crust of the buildings glistening in the yellow of streetlights. Beside them, the bronze statue wore a hat of snow and its base was worn shiny.

'St John of Nepomuk,' she read from her book. 'He was assassinated. Thrown into the river to drown.'

'Shitty ending.'

'But touching the statue is supposed to bring good luck.'

'Could always do with some of that.' Their fingers touched as both of them reached for the shiny surface. The bronze was cold, her fingers warm.

'You can make a wish.'

'What shall we wish for?' He was wishing he could kiss her.

She simply laughed.

'How about dinner?' he asked.

'I should get back. We both should.'

'Should we?' He wondered what Ryan and Tyler were up to. *Sod them!* They'd abandoned him last night.

'OK then. OK,' she said.

He picked a restaurant overlooking the Old Square – overpriced, but at least the menu was Italian and there was no risk of dumplings served with fatty, chewy pork. He ordered wine with the meal, allowing her preference for white, foregoing beer and a chaser beforehand. He drank no more than a glass and a half, aiming for a taste of it and only a small hazing over, just enough to stop himself examining too closely what it was that he was doing. They chatted easily, shifting into memories of childhood and adolescence, both of them avoiding – deliberately, or not, he wasn't sure – anything more recent. He could hardly ask if she had a boyfriend and not be prepared to answer the return question. She talked about her parents – both schoolteachers – and he talked about the embarrassment of his mum being a dinner lady, and his Dad always looking for work. 'A single child,' she said. 'I always wanted a sister.'

'I had a sister, a couple of years younger,' he said. 'But she died. A car accident. She was just thirteen.' He talked about the aftermath, his parents' frozen incomprehension. And how it was his mates who'd got him through with their clumsy unvoiced sympathy and carrying him home when he got too blottoed to walk.

'I'm sorry,' she said, her eyes wide with sympathy. 'It must have been tough. I don't suppose there's much anyone can say.'

'No.' He was grateful that she didn't try to.

They waited for the bill. She turned her mobile on. It bleeped and she messed around listening to messages. His fingers reached for his own phone, toying with the idea of doing the same; but then he couldn't face the conscience call of Selina on voicemail. 'Things are clearing. We may get on a flight tomorrow,' she said.

'That's a shame.'

She laughed. 'Don't be silly. We both have things to get back to.'

'I'm just beginning to enjoy it here.' He was enjoying the feel of life on hold, of drifting in the here and now.

'I'm enjoying it too. But it isn't real.'

'It could be.'

Her eyes met his, disconcerting him. Was what he'd said just a lousy chat-up line? Her raised eyebrows seemed to pose the question.

'I should get back,' she said.

'I'll walk with you.'

Their earlier talk gave way to quietness, as if they were done with chit-chat now and there was enough communication in the mingling of their misted breath and the alignment of their steps, sliding on the compacted snow.

'Here we are,' she said and slowed to a stop.

'Here we are.' Except he had no idea where they had got to. 'A nightcap? In the bar.'

Her eyes were serious and her answer slow. 'OK. In the bar,' she said.

He stepped up onto the curved step in front of the entrance to the hotel. His foot was already slipping as he noticed the black ice and his ankle gave way painfully beneath him.

'Oh God,' she said, a hand raised to cover up her laughter, and he realised he probably looked ridiculous, sprawling in the snow. His face contorted with pain and her expression switched guiltily to concern. 'Are you OK?' she asked, crouching down beside him.

'I'm fine,' he said. He pushed up, his weight half on one leg, a little on her, a little on his twisted ankle.

'Can you walk?'

'I don't know.'

'Better get you inside.'

He tried not to lean on her slight frame too heavily, tried not to give away how much it hurt.

He half-hobbled, half-hopped across the lobby. The bar was filled with a crush of loud-mouthed guys and she sighed before indicating the lifts. 'You can clean up upstairs.'

He smiled inwardly at the thought that if he'd been some sort of con-artist, he'd have achieved his aim. Was he a con-artist, he wondered, nothing but a sham?

The pain in his ankle was genuine.

'It couldn't be broken could it?'

'Doubt it.' He'd done this kind of thing before, playing football. The fact it felt bad didn't mean it was.

In her room, she took his coat and brushed it down, then deposited him on the bed. She removed her bulky outdoor clothes and he had a sense of her unwrapping her slender form for him. Not that it got further than her polo-necked jumper and jeans. She shook out her light-brown hair and it flowed down over her high firm breasts. He undid the lace of

15

his trainer, loosened it and eased it off. She brought a towel over and roughly rubbed his hair.

'How does it feel?'

'Feels good.'

She laughed, and with her face all alight she looked so beautiful. 'I meant your ankle.'

'I'll survive.' His hand moved upwards to cup her face and he could smell her citrus scent. The two of them looked at each other intently and his heart thumped with the thought: *this is it*. This was his chance to move things on and kiss her.

Then her eyes dipped away, and her face backed out from his palm. 'Simon,' she said. 'I've kept meaning to ask. You didn't say. Whose bachelor party is it?'

The moment's pause seemed to last forever and within it played out all sorts of lies. He'd intended to. All along in the background, he'd expected to lie. Lying often seemed to be his reflex.

Now it came to it, he couldn't bring himself to. Neither could he bear to tell the truth.

His silence clearly spoke the answer.

'OK,' she said quietly. 'OK.'

She stood up and moved away. 'Shall I ring you a cab?' she asked and she started to talk in a pointless way about how he might have to wait a while, what with the snow, but they seemed to manage well the cab-drivers didn't they, from what they'd seen.

'Katherine.'

'It's OK,' she said. 'Nothing happened. We said we'd have a day sightseeing and that's exactly what we did.'

'I didn't mean...'

'To deceive me? Well you haven't. I could have asked earlier and I didn't, but now I have and we both know where we stand.'

'I had a good time.'

'It's an interesting city.'

'That wasn't what I meant.'

'What do you mean then?' She turned, her face flushed, perhaps with the shift from cold to warm, perhaps with the transition into anger. 'Was I to be your last fling? Before you go back and marry your fiancée. When is the happy day anyway?'

'Next Saturday. And no, it isn't like that.'

'Or perhaps you're planning to ditch her days before the wedding on the basis of having had a nice time being tourists in Prague?'

He sat, head hung, because of course he didn't mean that either.

'I'll ring reception to get you a cab,' she said.

He put his sock back on and tested out the joint. It was fine, just it would be painful for a bit. He wondered if he'd be able to walk down the aisle without limping. Except it was the bride on whom all eyes would be focussed, as she swept down the aisle towards him, in the dress that she had chosen above all others and which to him would look identical to every single wedding dress he had ever, in his entire life, seen. He wondered quite what it was about Selina which meant that out of the steady stream of one night stands and casually dating someone for a week, a month or several, she had been the one to stick.

Katherine accompanied him out of her room and towards the lifts. In reception, they occupied seats near the door, and he felt the blast of cold every time someone came or went. Neither of them said anything.

He stood as a cab drew up outside and she got up too and came out with him. At the last moment, he turned and she allowed him to kiss her, neither deflecting him, nor actively responding, so it remained half chaste, half something closer.

The cab drove slowly through the brown sludge of snow. The car passed a group of women, dressed up in heels and short skirts, singing lustily and swaying. He tried to think of the wedding on Saturday and everybody being there and he wondered how, when it actually came to it, he'd feel.

All he could feel now was frozen.

Differences in Lifts

– Lander Hawes –

In the office where I work there are two lifts, positioned next to each other at the rear of the lobby. For a long time I assumed they were both identical in every way; their design is identical, and they are machines, and as we all know, there should be little or no variation in the working processes of identical machines.

After a few months of using the lifts daily, I began to notice that the lift on the right had a door that closed more quickly and forcefully than the door of the lift on the left.

'The door on this lift is dangerous,' I said to Paul, my colleague from the marketing department, one day when we were riding up in the right hand lift together.

'Oh is it? Fucking typical,' he said.

Then, a few days, or a few weeks or even months later, I entered this lift holding a mug of tea. I'd just made this mug of tea, and it was scalding hot, and as I stepped across the threshold of the lift the door closed and knocked my arm, making me throw the hot liquid forwards, narrowly missing a girl standing at the back by the mirror.

The door of the left hand lift could never have done this.

It was around this time that the county council changed the health and safety regulations, and we all had to start carrying buckets of water. The council even provided the buckets, stainless steel ones that could never be mistaken for a normal garden or domestic bucket. Oh no. These buckets clanked properly when set down on the hard tiles that pave the corridors and atrium spaces of the office, and the water slopped about in a very pleasing way whenever anyone tried to walk too fast with one. The trick, we all decided, was only to half fill them.

One day I saw Paul arguing with one of the managers.

'You should really have your bucket,' the manager said.

'Oh for chrissakes. It's such a stupid rule,' Paul said.

'What if there's a fire?' the manager asked.

'One bucket won't make a difference.'

'What if everyone took that attitude? Then we'd have no water at all!'

'Well I'm taking that attitude.'

Of course it wasn't really Paul's fault that the government had disbanded the fire service, and that now we were all meant to take responsibility for our own fires, but there you go.

That evening Paul and I went out for a drink in town. We sat in a bar along the high street, and looked out of the window at the people passing by, who were mainly teenagers and tourists.

'Bloody buckets,' Paul said.

'They're being more strict about it.'

'For god's sake, why can't just half the office carry them?'

He was folding up a beer mat with both his hands, forcing the cardboard into an ever smaller cube.

'What, like a shift system?'

'Something like that.'

'The company ought to pay for some fire attendants.'

'I know. But they won't will they?'

We glanced at each other knowingly and sipped our drinks.

Then there was a commotion outside. Some teenagers sprinted down the high street, running pretty hard. They looked a little underfed and neglected. A police car was pursuing them, but only slowly because of all the traffic calming measures, like sponge curtains the cars had to force their way through, and the fluorescent seesaw they had to go over. Then a police van came from the other direction, and we watched the teenagers get arrested and taken away. It was clear that they'd strayed into a higher credit zone than they could afford, or that they'd stayed too long in a luxury credit zone and their accounts had depleted to zero.

I felt sorry for them. It's easy to forget where the boundaries for the different zones in the town centre are. Of course it's true that the police are at an advantage, because they have access to everyone's GPS locaters. Really, there should be a system where people are warned when they enter a luxury zone, and told how much the minute by minute charge rate is. But there you go.

'I think I'm going to talk to the management about the lifts.'

Paul didn't answer at first. He was watching the police van drive away.

'What?'

'The dangerous lift door at work?'

'Oh. Yeah. Someone needs to sort that out,' he said.

He kept staring as the van disappeared around a corner. I watched with him.

'There's a lot that needs to be sorted out,' he continued, almost to himself.

Then he turned round to look at me and I smiled.

'Do you want another drink?' I asked.

The next day, in the early afternoon, I was half way through a weekly repetitive fantasy workshop. The counsellor, a visiting therapist called Gail, was sitting on the floor in the middle of a circle of cross-legged employees. We'd all taken our shoes off, and were wearing our therapy loincloths. Most people had left their buckets by the door, but mine was by my toes. One of the office cleaners, Hussein, was talking.

'Definitely, when I'm cleaning the second floor, I think about different things than when I'm cleaning the ground.'

'Are we talking about thinking or fantasizing, Hussein?' Gail asked.

'Oh right yeah no it's fantasizing, that's what I meant.'

'Can anyone remind us of the difference?'

I put up my hand.

'Thank you, Miles.'

'Thinking is directed thought, whereas fantasizing is involuntary and reactive thought.'

'That's pretty good, yes thank you, Miles.'

'Well when I'm cleaning on the second floor I fantasize about terrorists attacking the building, I fantasize about what I'd do, like throwing a table over the balcony at them when they rush into the reception.'

'Good.'

'And I think about how easy it would be to block the lifts, so they'd have to come up the stairs.'

'And how do you manage these fantasies, Hussein?'

Hussein sniffed.

'I tell myself they're just a coping mechanism, like you say, just the brain mucking about because it hasn't anything better to do.'

'Marvellous.'

There was a knock on the door. We all looked round. One of the managers was peering round the opened door.

'Sorry to interrupt everyone. Something's come up; Miles, could I have a word?'

'Oh excuse me,' I said.

I stood, picked up my bucket, and went to talk to the manager in the corridor outside.

'Hi,' I said.

'Miles, listen something has happened. Paul's been arrested and he's named you as a supporting witness. The police want you to go down to the station. They need to interview you.'

The manager put his hands on his hips. He was a very tall man, and in that moment his size made me feel as if he were a deputy headmaster who had extracted me from a lesson, and I a pupil bewildered by the interruption to my routine.

'God, that is weird. I'd best drive down there.'

'I know Paul's been troubled and unstable recently, and frankly we've been well, concerned about him, but I don't think anyone ever expected anything like this.'

He looked closely at me and sighed. He frowned, which was strange, as he wasn't a man that frowned often.

'Right.'

'Between you and I, Miles, it might be best if you tell me all the details tomorrow. Try to keep your distance a little too. I know he's your friend, but, you know. I mean, he's put us all in a very difficult position.'

'Well, I'll be as professional as I can.'

I started off down the corridor.

'Miles?'

I turned round; the manager pointed at my loin-clothed crotch.

'Best change first.'

'Oh. Oh yeah.'

I hurried away.

The police station reception was very crowded and noisy. There must have been almost a hundred people roaming about in the forum area, the sound of their chatting and shouting mixing with the frequent announcements from the tannoy. After I'd queued for an hour the police interviewed me. It was very dull. They wanted to know if I'd been out with Paul the night before and what we'd seen. But the good thing was they said they might release Paul that evening; only they had to consult with the magistrate first.

Afterwards I was given a code and then had to wait for one of the consoles to be free. By the time I managed to sit down and key in the code for Paul's cell-cam it was almost five o'clock.

'Hello Paul.'

The screen showed him sitting on the metal bench in his cell. He looked haggard and unwell, like he'd been vomiting.

'Miles. Thank God. The cunts really fucked me up.'

He spoke slowly, his voice sounding hoarse and rasping.

'Are you injured?'

'They gassed me last night. I've got to get out of here and speak to a solicitor.'

'God. What happened?'

'I came down about those lads that were arrested. You remember from last night?'

'Of course, yes.'

Paul looked at the floor and shifted his position on the bench, inclining to one side and putting more of his weight onto his right arm. He spent some hesitant moments taking a deep breath, as if the breathing made his throat or lungs uncomfortable. Staring at the floor, and with effort, he went on talking.

'I told the police I was the dad of one of the boys and I paid their fines. Then the police did a DNA test and charged me with attempted kidnap.'

'Let's talk about it on the drive back.'

He nodded, still staring at the floor.

'Thing is mate, I've had enough.'

'Well, you're not alone. The problem is here, neither are we.'

He took a while to reply, and I wondered if the police had used some medication on him, one of those sedative sprays, the kind they use to facilitate dialogue.

'Yeah, anything you say and all that.'

'What you need is some proper legal representation.'

'This feels like the beginning of something, really like a beginning.'

He looked at the camera, and his face seemed set and firmed up, in contrast to the disgruntled and disenchanted slackness it had acquired in recent months.

'Are you with me, Miles?'

'Paul, I'm your friend. Let's talk in the car.'

In the end I waited about half an hour in the cafe. I barely had time to finish my cappuccino, of which all profits went to the police retirement fund, before Paul was brought out to the reception. He had to pay a fine with his card, and when he'd completed the disclaimer and detainee feedback forms I put my arm around his shoulders and helped him out to the car.

'You smell a bit,' I said, once we were underway.

'I pissed myself when they gassed me.'

About halfway back to town I stopped the car. I walked around to the other side and opened Paul's door.

'Paul, I'm going to have to ask you to get out.'

He stared at me, and I kept looking right back at him, polite but firm.

'I don't smell that bad, mate. We can open a window if you like.'

Then he frowned a bit but unbuckled his seatbelt and swung his feet onto the tarmac.

'The police have punished you, Paul, but as your friend and colleague, I feel I should punish you again. It's for you own good. I've driven you half way, because I like you, but you're going to have to walk the rest.'

He was struggling to speak. His narrow, bony face appeared about to spasm.

'Miles, what?'

'You'll thank me one day.'

I walked around to my side of the car, got in, and drove off. I watched him in the rear view mirror doing up the zip of his jacket. He had definitely got thinner during his night in the cells.

Hang Up

– Shanta Everington –

Ian stares at the words on the screen, waiting for the phone to ring. His chin rests on his palms, his elbows on the desk. Eyes blur. Elbows buzz. It's been nearly two hours. He sighs and leans back; refocusing and stretching out his legs, letting his head roll. He's glad to be on shift alone tonight. Not strictly by the rules but what with the new girl being sacked for internet dating on duty, and Graham off with his guts again, he doesn't like to let anybody down. The men in suits aren't happy with the stats as it is. And besides, Marjorie said he could ring her mobile any time if he needed to debrief. He thinks of the new girl. All eyebrow rings and attitude. A year older than Lisa.

He closes his eyes and sees the letter from Sarah. Twenty-three years reduced to ink on paper. Real ink, like always. He laughs a silent laugh, rolling his pen between forefinger and thumb, craving a smoke.

Dear Ian, I think you should get a solicitor.

Biro between lips, he takes a draw before walking over to the sink to refill the kettle. He could do with a scotch but it's been nearly two years and he's proud of that.

Irreconcilable differences.

Maybe he should get his head down for a bit and blank out. Will anyone call now? He needs to be ready. It's not about him now.

Somewhere across the city, in the darkness, Sarah tosses in her bed, eyes open, thinking about what she had and what she lost, wondering if she'll ever sleep again. A few doors down, a stubbled man in a suit comes home late, smelling of booze and staggers up the stairs.

Another town. Another woman. She lies on top of the bed covers, listening to Premier radio. God is going to help her through. She reaches out to her bedside table and her hand hovers over the phone.

Ian pours hot water on coffee granules and stirs, listening to the clink of metal against china. He cradles the mug in both hands, looking at the picture. A cuddly bear, just visible, faded over the years from washing. *Dear Dad.*

The phone rings. Shrill and unexpected. The coffee spills. He scrabbles back to the desk and slips on his headset, scratching his cheek.

'I'm listening.'

'You sound like a nice man. What's your name?' A high pitched jolly female voice. Perhaps early thirties.

'We're not allowed to give out our names on this helpline.' He tries to make his voice sound friendly. But rules should be obeyed.

'Oh, sorry, sorry. My name's Anne. Am I allowed to say that? Are you allowed to call me by my name?'

'That's fine, Anne. So, what would you like to talk about?'

'Oh. So how will I get to speak to you again, then? Do you always work on Thursday nights? Is this your regular shift?'

'Any of my colleagues will be able to help if you need to talk to someone again.'

'You've got a nice voice. You remind me of my father.'

You were a lousy father.

'Would you like to talk about your father?'

'It's cold today, isn't it? Not in here though. I've got the heating up full. Warm as toast. That's what he used to say. Warm as toast. Do they let you put the heating on there or are they tight with the budget?'

'It's fine here. So you're thinking about your father.' Ian pinches the bridge of his nose. This is Anne's father. Anne's father. Anne. Not Lisa.

'But is it too hot in there? You know it can be just as bad if the heating's too high, can't it? Then it's all stuffy and sweaty and horrible.'

'You don't like it being too hot.'

'No.'

Silence.

'I'm listening, Anne.'

'Oh.' Giggles. 'I like you saying Anne. Can you say it again?'

'You like to hear me say your name. I'm wondering why that might be.'

'Yes, so can you say it again?'

'I'm wondering why you want me to say your name?'

'Don't worry about it. So, are you wearing a jumper?'

'It's not important what I'm wearing. Let's get back to what you want to talk about.'

'But I want to know. That's what I want to talk about.'

'We're not here to talk about me. We're here to talk about you.'

'I'm wearing a jumper. It's pink with grey flowers.'

Silence.

'And I'm wearing dungarees.'

Silence.

'And boots. I bet you are wearing a jumper.'

Silence.

'You don't say much do you?'

'I'm listening.'

'I think it might snow again tomorrow.'

'You think it might snow.'

'Yeah.'

'So how do you feel about that?'

Laughs. 'How do I feel about the snow? I'm not bothered.'

'Did you phone up to talk about the snow or is there something else on your mind?' Shit. A bit confrontational. Marjorie only told him last week in supervision that he needed to give the caller more space instead of jumping in too quickly with questions.

Sighs.

'I don't think you phoned to talk about the weather, did you?' He can't help himself.

'You don't know that. You don't know what I called for so don't say that!'

'OK, OK. I'm listening to whatever you want to say.' Breathe.

'My dad always wore jumpers. Even in the summer. Why do you think that is?'

Lisa loved you so much and you failed her.

'I don't know. Why do you think it might be?'

'He didn't like his arms out. He liked to be covered up.'

'Your dad liked to be covered up.'

'Yes. So are you going to ask me some questions now?'

'You're wondering if I am going to ask you questions.'

'So are you?'

'I'm here to listen.' He sees Marjorie in her floaty floral skirt by the flip chart, talking about the Victim-Rescuer-Perpetrator triangle. But he can't remember what it means.

'Are you playing a game with me?' Giggles.

Serious. Calm. 'No, I'm not playing a game. I'm listening to what you have to say. Shall we talk some more about your father?'

I don't think you even knew what being a father was about, Ian, I really don't.

'Oh, OK. What do you want to know?'

'What would you like to say about him?'

Silence.

'Anne?'

'Hi.' Giggles.

Silence.

'I'm listening.'

'He liked to keep his boots on, all the time, even when he was inside. He used to make a joke about it. I'll die with my boots on!'

'I've noticed that you're talking about you father in the past tense.'

Jesus, you didn't even cry at her funeral, Ian.

'Ten out of ten, Mister Man With No Name.'

Silence.

'He's past tense.' Pause. 'Past. I like that word.'

'You like the word "past".'

'Finished. Over. The end. No more.'

'It sounds as though you're talking about something that's very important to you.'

34

You never got your priorities right.

'Hmm. But if it does snow, there'll be chaos. The train's will be all messed up, won't they?'

'I'm wondering if you need to take a train somewhere?'

'You wonder a lot of things, don't you, Mister! Mind your own business.' Laughing. 'Do you need to take a train somewhere?'

Silence.

'Do you need to take a train to wherever you are? Will you be able to make your next shift? Will there be anyone on the helpline?'

'Yes, I'm sure the helpline will stay open if it snows.'

'The smallest little thing and the trains go berserk, don't they? Like a leaf on the line! Have you ever heard anything so absurd?!' Laughing. 'How can a leaf stop a train? Now a body under a train. That's something else.'

'A body under the train is something else.'

'You sound like a parrot. Is that how they teach you to talk? Just to be a parrot? Can't you talk like a real person? Jesus. I might as well talk to my tape recorder and play it back to myself.'

His heart is beating too fast. 'I'm wondering how you're feeling right now, Anne.'

'Don't fucking call me Anne. I'm angry. Fucking angry at the stupid way you're fucking talking to me, you cunt. How dare you call me Anne when you won't fucking give me your name?'

Breathe. Remember to breathe. The girl, Kayla, is in tears as she flees, wipes her snot on the back of her hand. She was only checking her messages, she says quietly as she passes Ian. Marjorie stands in her office doorway, hands on hips, then disappears behind a closed door to eat a sandwich and a bag of crisps. Breathe. Remember to breathe.

'It's OK. I won't use your name again. It's OK to be angry.'

The sound of gasps.

'I'm sorry. Are you going to put the phone down on me?'

'No, I'm not going to put the phone down on you. I'm going to listen to you.'

'I'm sorry. I didn't mean to get angry. Please don't think I'm a bad person.'

'I don't think you're a bad person.'

A whisper: 'But, but, how do you know?'

'I've no reason to think you are bad.'

Silence. Then shallow breathing.

A little girl's voice: 'But you don't know that do you?'

'I'm wondering what you think or feel about yourself?'

'I hate myself.'

Sometimes I hate you.

'Do you want to tell me why you hate yourself?'

I wonder how you can live with yourself after everything you've done.

'No, I don't.'

'OK.'

'I think I'm going to go now.'

'You think you're going to go.'

'Hmm.'

'Are you going to say goodbye?' Giggles.

'Do you want to end the call, Anne?'

Giggles. 'You are playing a game now, aren't you?'

'No. I'm asking whether you want to end the call, Anne?'

'I thought you weren't going to call me Anne?'

Shit. 'I'm sorry. Do you want to end the call?'

'Why did you call me Anne?'

'I'm sorry I forgot.'

You were a lousy father to Lisa when she was alive. Why would I want you now she's dead?

'Oh. But you're not allowed to do stuff like that, are you, Mister Man?'

Ian closes his eyes. His fingers find the scratch on his cheek. Touch wetness. 'I suppose it just shows that nobody's perfect. It's OK to make mistakes sometimes.'

'Is it though?'

'Yes. It's OK.'

'Not always though. Some mistakes are bad, aren't they? Some things mean you're evil, don't they?'

'Evil's a strong word.'

'But there is evil, isn't there?'

'You think there is evil.'

'Some things are evil, aren't they?'

'Different people have different views on what evil means. I'm wondering what it means to you?'

'Some people are bad though, aren't they?'

'I'm wondering if you might be talking about anyone in particular?'

Silence.

'What if I did something bad?'

'I'm wondering if you think you did something bad?'

'What if I did? Am I evil?'

'No. If you did something bad, it doesn't mean that you are a bad person. Everyone…'

Screaming: 'Don't say 'everyone makes mistakes!' Like that makes it OK.'

Ian feels his heart expanding. As though it might explode through his rib cage and splatter across the smudged files on his desk. 'OK. OK. I'm wondering if we are talking about you doing something bad or someone else.'

Hang up.

'Fuck!' Ian kicks the leg of the desk. His temples throb. His eyes sting. His shoulders ache. He pulls off the headset and goes to grab the mug of coffee, pouring it down the sink.

He thinks of Anne at home in her dungarees and grey jumper with pink flowers.

He thinks of Anne's father and wonders what happened.

He thinks he probably said all the wrong things.

He thinks of Lisa the last time he saw her. Home from college for the summer looking happy.

He thinks of the therapist telling him what he felt when he felt nothing.

He thinks of Sarah. The woman he once loved. Still loves.

He thinks of the daughter he will never see again.

He thinks of nothing.

Anne is trembling as she replaces the receiver. Her breathing is coming hard.

'Bastard!' she screams.

There is a knock on the wall.

'Keep it down in there. People are trying to sleep.'

'So am I,' she whispers and pulls back the covers. She takes off her dirty off-white dressing gown and throws it across the room, before getting in the bed naked.

The bedside light is still on. It shines brightly reflecting against the glass in the photo frame. Anne stares at it but all she can see is the beam of light, hurting her eyes.

There is Anne, aged six, sitting at the top of the slide in the playground, wearing dungarees over a grey jumper with pink flowers, her boots pointing towards the camera. She is smiling at her father as he tells her to say 'cheese' and clicks the button. She'll always be his special girl.

The radio is still playing quietly. God is love. God is good. God is beauty. Praise him.

Gottle O' Geer

– Melissa Mann –

It's decided. From now on I'll be inseparable from a ball of wool in case
the urge to knit should overwhelm me at any point during the course of
my day. Above us, the sun shines loudly in a sky silent but for the odd
remark of cloud. Carlsberg o'clock by my reckoning. Had I not been
sacked, I'd be in the gents round about now, drinking the first of my
twelve-a-day, necking one down while my supervisor moves his bowels in
the cubicle next to me. Happy days. Used to hide my cans in the cistern –
a kind of improvised cool-box, if you will. Ingenious I thought rather
than grounds for dismissal, but then what do I know about genius? I'm a
Smith. We Smiths tend to live as we die, in our sleep, which is why I
resent having to come here of course. Being an alcoholic is my one claim
to a personality. Without it I'd be dull as ditchwater like all the rest.

'I finished my amends last night,' says Tony, hands stuffed in the
pockets of his shorts.

I look away. Tony's a sex addict, that's why he's here. Unfortunately
me knowing this about him gives everything he does a sexual
connotation. Yesterday in the canteen he asked me to pass the
mayonnaise and I'm afraid I had to leave the table.

We're all clapping Tony's achievement. Well I say we, I'm clapping
with my smile, hands otherwise engaged passing loops of green wool
between two knitting needles. Idle work for devil hands.

'Please, please,' says Tony, holding up his palms to quell the applause.

'What did you do with the amends you can't send?' says Miranda, a petite woman with quite the biggest breasts I've ever laid eyes on. When she cries – something she does often and without warning – I imagine her lactating, for some reason. I can't help it.

Miranda is a blushing widow who has sought solace from her grief at partypoker.com.

'I put mine in Charles' urn at the back of the airing cupboard. Charles and I shared everyth…oh…sorry…'

See, never any warning. I reach forward and offer a handkerchief to her breasts.

'It's a good question, Miranda,' says Tony, taking his hands out of his pockets.

What can I say, it's a relief.

'The amends I can't send I rolled into a tube…' he says, squinting through the hole he's made with his hand, '…then I shoved my cock through it,' and he thrusts his pelvis forward. 'It seemed appropriate somehow.'

We're laughing. Well, I say we, I'm laughing with my eyes, brain otherwise engaged with the task of not thinking about Tony's penis…a task I see Claire and Kathy are grappling with too. Claire has Obsessive-Compulsive Disorder, the official term ascribed to her condition by the medical profession. Claire, in her infinite wisdom, prefers to call her OCD Kathy. She's sitting opposite me now, wearing a shirt so white with new it deafens all who gaze upon it.

'Cocks and sneezes spread diseases,' she says to Tony disapprovingly, wringing Kathy's hands.

I drop a stitch.

Tony stands up and gestures lewdly at his fly. 'Come and have a go if you think I'm not hard enough,' he goads.

Claire turns away. Her face looks like it's been shot. Tony laughs then leaves the art therapy class, taking the papier-mâché goat he's just made with him. It's nearly eleven thirty. Time for his one-to-one with Dr Rendell.

Now there's just the six of us. Miranda and Claire I mentioned earlier. Then there's Robert, the bulimic, Rachel who can't stop buying crap from Argos, and Owen who is new and yet to reveal. Going by the impressive cannabis leaf tattoos he's got creeping ivy-like over his arms and back, my money's on some kind of substance abuse. Could be wrong of course. I never was much of a gambler...not compared to Simon anyway. He's the eighth member of our merry band, and spectacularly addicted to William Hill. I look at the pause in the circle where Simon usually sits. He was sent to his room ten minutes ago to change his clothes, the *Sex and Drugs and Sausage Rolls* t-shirt he was wearing deemed unnecessarily provocative by the rest of the group.

'We've a good mind to tell Dr Rendell about Tony,' says Claire, scratching Kathy's neck irritably. 'We won't put up with being sexually harassed like that.'

'Well it was you what brought up his cock being diseased,' says Robert, sniffing a crayon then inexplicably licking the end of it.

'Yes, you did rather ask for it,' says Miranda, looking earnestly at Claire from the depths of her breasts.

I lean back against the tree, suddenly overcome by a bone-dissolving weariness. Shielding my eyes from the sun, I look round the group. What a strange collection of people we are. Have I made them up, I wonder, or have they made me up? Beautiful place this though, I'll give the wife that. I look out across the surrounding fields, at the yellow, green, brown squares stitched together with neat hedgerows. Very humbling, nature, I've always thought. There's something about the infinity of arable crops that makes me feel incredibly small and insignificant. I hug my knees.

'What are you doing, Owen?' says Rachel, looking over the top of her sunglasses. 'Or shouldn't I ask?'

Arranged between his fingers, three cigarettes. Rachel's eyes flit from his hand to the honed muscle of his naked torso. "Ripped" I think is the term *Men's Health* would use to describe him. Apparently Rachel has pledged to bed the poor fellow before the week is out. That's the word on the strasse anyway. I imagine it will be a rather shuddering, clingy kind of fuck, such is the scale of Rachel's neediness.

Owen starts lighting the cigarettes, a slow, precise kind of firing up. He's using a cheap novelty lighter with a curvy cartoon blonde on the side who magically loses her swimsuit when the thing is upended.

'Only smoke three fags a day, yeah,' says Owen, sucking on the filtered ends. The sound is not unlike a vacuum choking on a curtain. 'Each one represents the women in me life who've made me the way I am now – me mam, me ex-wife and me last girlfriend,' he says, pointing at each cigarette in turn. He blows a large smoke ring pause. 'So every day, what I do, yeah, is set fire to the lot of 'em. It's kind of like a ritual.'

Rachel coughs then busies herself looking for nothing in her mock Next handbag.

I smile at Owen and start to cast off. Dr Rendell is going to have a field day with that one. At last, a proper mentalist to get his teeth into. As for me, I'm rather a disappointment to the good doctor on that score. I confuse him with my multiple choice answers. The problem is I have absolutely no respect for his profession. To my mind, no one has the right to change another human being, which rather means psychotherapy as a concept is fundamentally flawed of course. And as for the "twelve-step abstinence-based therapeutic model" he uses, forget it. I'm a church-*fearing* man. I believe only one thing – there is no Power greater than me, which means God too, as a concept, is fundamentally flawed. Anyway, I prefer to bat for the other team, it's more fun.

As you can imagine then, my own one-to-one sessions with Rendell are a complete joke. We just sit opposite each other talking in the language of road signs. Rendell fails to grasp one very simple fact about my drinking – I do it because it makes me who I'm meant to be. I drink to excess to feel the things I should feel when I'm sober, but for some reason don't. Without alcohol, I'm nothing, a non-entity. Beer makes me a proper functioning human being. A man with emotions, who's actually capable of expressing them. When I drink it's like I'm standing in the middle of a model village; I feel more real, more alive.

'You're deluding yourself, Alan,' Rendell said when I tried to explain this to him. 'The reality is, every time you drink beer, you're killing yourself.'

'Oh don't be so dramatic,' I replied, wiping my mouth. 'It's a sad fact of life, doctor, the things that kill you are the very things that make you feel most alive. Drugs, alcohol, fast cars, prostitutes. Which is why I have grave reservations about this God of yours and the so-called *love* he has for his flock.' I fingered my copy of the Serenity Prayer. 'Anyway, it's quality of life, not quantity, in my view. And it feels good to be out of control. Really good in fact.' I looked at the fastidious crease down the front of his trousers. 'Not that you would know this. Seriously, doctor, you might want to try it some time.'

'And your wife, Alan? Your work colleagues? All the people who have to deal with you when you're out of control? Do you think it feels good to them?'

Ah yes, the guilty card. The only real weapon Rendell has at his disposal.

'Your wife loves you very much, Alan, but she hates your drinking.' He leaned forward in his seat. 'Do you ever wonder what it must be like for her, watching you kill yourself like this? Don't you love your wife, Alan?'

I stood up. 'Let's be clear, doctor, the man Sandra loves is the one she married twenty-six years and two months ago, and alas that's not who I really am. As for loving her,' I said, staring out the window. 'I love the part of my wife that hates me but won't let the rest of her admit it.'

And that's the only interesting exchange we've had in ten days, Rendell and I. The very first session. All the ones since have been a complete waste of time – a half-hearted attempt by Rendell to dig me up with a question or two, then a few very ordinary lies that sound vaguely like the truth, from me by way of response.

'What are you knitting, Alan? Legwarmers?' asks Miranda, plucking the front of her t-shirt.

I look at the length of green wool I'm sewing up to form a tube. 'Errm, sort of, Miranda.'

'My Gran used to wear legwarmers, but on her arms though,' says Robert, shoving up his sleeves with the food shovels he calls hands. 'Wore 'em all the time. Even made us promise to bury her in 'em. It was in her will an' everything.'

'That reminds me,' says Owen, brutally stubbing out a fag on the sole of his Doc Marten. 'There was a programme on the telly the other night before I come 'ere. It were going on about 'ow the last sense to leave you before yer die is yer 'earing.'

'Really?' I say, tying off the wool. 'How did they work that out?'

'Dunno,' says Owen, wiping his nose on the back of his hand. 'Science, wan't it. Went over me 'ead. Got expelled when I were thir'een for settin' fire to a lass's plait wi' a Bunsen burner. Never went back after that.'

'Right...fascinating. Hearing though, you say. Well that's unfortunate.' I put my knitting away. 'Means I can look forward to departing this mortal coil to the dulcet tones of my wife saying, "I told you it'd kill you, Alan."'

'Oh, but you're doing so well, isn't he, Kathy?' says Claire, rubbing the front of her shirt repeatedly.

I get to my feet and look towards the main building. 'Right, going to have to love you and leave you,' I say, addressing my fellow inmates. 'Need to see a man about a dog...'

…or rather a cleaner about a six-pack. I set off across the lawn in the direction of my room.

According to the alarm clock, it's 11.54. I'm sitting on the bed, trying to occupy my trembling hands with the task of sorting through the knitted tubes. How odd they look lined up that way – like little woolly body bags. 11.55. I squeeze my hands into fists trying to wring out the tremor. Clock, door, hands. Ludmila, Ludmila, wherefore art thou Ludmila?

I was barely an hour into this 14-day detox retreat when I discovered you can have way too much of not enough. Enter Ludmila. She's Croatian or Bulgarian or…anyway, she's a cleaner here, working for what can only be described as a pittance. So, in the spirit of you-scratch-my-back-I'll-scratch-yours, I offered to supplement the funds she sends home to her sick mother in Bregana or Velingrad or wherever, in return for her doing a spot of illicit shopping for me.

A squeaking, tapping noise in the corridor outside. Wheels and heels – how big, how beautiful the sound!

'Hull-o, how are you being?' says Ludmila lyrically, her bulk framed by the doorway. Not waiting for a reply, she heaves a black plastic sack off her cart and drags it behind her into the room like a dead elk. 'Here is shopping,' she stage-whispers, looking over her shoulder, then closes the door. 'Twelve Carlingbergs. I am keeping them for you in cooling bag.'

'Very thoughtful, Ludmila, thank you,' I say, opening my wallet.

'There is being porno too, here in bag. Is for Tony. You know this mans? Big Tony in next door. Perhaps you are wanting this DVDs also? Is *Clitty Clitty Gang Bang*. Very great porno, so Tony is telling me.'

Tempting, I like a good musical. Best not though. I shake my head, handing her a bunch of notes in exchange for the two six-packs she's holding out in her fists. Big hands – I'm thinking maybe gender correction surgery sometime in the distant past.

'We do more bizniz on the mornings, yes?' she says, tucking the notes in her bra.

'Definitely. Best make it eighteen though, Ludmila. Got the wife coming tomorrow for a visit. Might need a spot of Danish courage beforehand,' I say, tapping the side of my nose.

Ludmila nods solemnly. 'Okay, yes. I bring three six-packets. Bye-bye,' she says and leaves the room.

I'm kneeling in front of the mirror now – how comfortable we Smiths are on our knees! – waiting to confront myself with the personality I acquire through the glory of beer. I've got one can tucked in the front pocket of my cords, the other I'm holding like the mittened hand of a child who's about to run out into the road. I say mittened because the can is wearing one of the knitted covers I made in art therapy. They all are in fact. Ten beers lined up here on the floor in matching woolly body bags. I raise the can aloft, toast myself in the mirror, then neck it down as fast as I can.

The Swan King

– Ashley Stokes –

This will be the last time that he sees her. He will be in Milan, in the Piazza Fontana. Her head will rest on the shoulder of a tall, grey-haired man. In his unstructured jacket and frameless glasses, the grey-haired man will have the air of a business consultant or European media executive. Slender still, she will be wearing a bronze-coloured leather coat and high suede boots and be tanned even though it is winter. They will be holding hands and will laugh as they stride across the piazza. Adrian will not be alone in noticing them. Everyone else in the piazza, the bystanders and tourists will pause and watch them as they head towards the cathedral.

The familiar twinge will pulse behind his eyes. In crowds, Adrian is still goaded, even after all this time, by the faces of people he once knew. He will always be mistaken and often embarrassed and ashamed by this. In Milan he will not have time to wonder why he keeps thinking he sees her.

This time it is her.

They strut past him. They are talking Italian. Beneath the accent, her voice that he now vividly remembers from the room is still there, husky and saddening. He knows it would be reckless, catastrophic even, to introduce himself, let alone follow them. It had all happened twenty years ago, when he was more than capable of following someone about. He

51

will be able to use the length of the sentence to count the years, backwards to the days after Elaine Preece had disappeared.

Δ

Twenty years ago she had been missing for five days. Her disappearance had reached the national news bulletins and the front pages of the tabloids. That morning, after reports of the massacre of pro-democracy protestors in Beijing it was the second item on the *Today Programme*. Mounting fears for the safety of a second-year undergraduate not seen since…A statement from her frantic boyfriend was followed by a police request for information however trivial. Adrian, then a second-year undergraduate himself was making plans and mental lists. The evening was a long way off. He would be useless until then.

Outside, a peculiar tension spoilt the summer ambience. Students speculated on the steps of libraries, in college gatehouses, on the quads and in refectories behind curtain-walls and Portland stone, in the cafes that Adrian passed. He could hear them whisper her name. He was alone, he felt, in not claiming a past intimacy with Elaine Preece.

Last night, Gareth Llewellyn, who lived in the room below, had waylaid Adrian on the step. Some weeks before, he'd seen Elaine Preece in the Jazz Cellar. She was sucking a tequila sunrise through a straw and giving him the eye even though her hulking American boyfriend gripped her tiny hand.

'Gagging, she was, Addo, I tell you, gagging for it.'

By then Adrian's tutorial partner, Hannah Mitchelmore had already explained over coffee that she too knew Elaine Preece. They had organized a Rag Week parade together. 'She's nice, friendly. Beautiful eyes. She never simpers.' 'Simper' was the word Hannah used to dismiss almost all of female kind. It was only later that Adrian realized. This was the same girl that Zara had told him about, the one Anthony Christmas was bragging that he'd 'tupped half to death' after a Law Society disco.

'But he plays lacrosse,' Zara had said during Sunday lunch. 'Have you ever met anyone who plays lacrosse who isn't excruciatingly dishonest?'

Adrian had never met anyone who played lacrosse, but was prepared, in this instance, to accept Zara's reasoning as Scientific Method.

Other than Anthony and the low-down antics of his brother Hugo Christmas, who had once represented the London School of Economics at lacrosse and was now in Ford Open Prison for insider trading, Zara had mainly talked about the disappearance of Elaine Preece. Afterwards, Adrian feared that she'd only said yes to tonight because the fate of her great friend Elaine Preece had distracted her. Otherwise she would have discretely but firmly batted away the suggestion like she would a money spider scaling her wrist.

Zara Gregory was coming to his room tonight. Zara Gregory: a.k.a. The Heartbreaker. Beneath her feet, pavements shimmered. Every swing of her hips or flick of her hair reversed the slow orbits of a hundred Gareths and Anthonys. She was coming to Adrian's room this evening; he assumed to hang out, drink wine and play records, not just talk about her Kant essay. He didn't want to go through all of this just to end up writing an essay for her. The undertow of a terrible current dragged at his guts. The last three days had felt like the time before an exam he knew he would fail however much he revised. He had stressed over a girl like this once before. That girl was the last person he should be thinking about now. That girl needed to be kept in a drawer, or a strongbox or bunker. She needed to be kept away. She wasn't even a girl anymore.

He found himself in a shopping centre. As he approached Eternal Flame, the candle shop, he was again reliving a moment after Sunday lunch when they were paused in the street outside The Eagle and Child and she'd whispered, 'Yes, I'd love to come'. He knew then he would have to buy candles and line them up around his shelves and dim the lights and play the sort of music girls like.

Outside Eternal Flame, a dumpy woman in a denim shirt that didn't match her darker, mottled jeans crouched in front of a pushchair. For no reason, the dumpy woman looked away from her child to stare up at him. She knew.

It wasn't until he was back outside that he felt himself again. There would be no candles now.

In HMV he browsed the aisles for music that girls like. Zara could be the sort of girl who only listens to Satie and Rachmaninoff; or she might like the bafflingly fashionable robot-on-piano music played in nightclubs. She hadn't said anything about music over lunch, or when they'd met for a drink last week, or during that fateful coffee break after they'd started to chat in the Upper Reading Room.

Patsy Cline. He'd buy something by Patsy Cline. He didn't know anything about Patsy Cline but remembered a drama on ITV in which a tall, suave man got this nice blonde girl back to his flat. He'd lined dozens of birthday cake candles along his bookshelves and was playing a song that Adrian's mother said was sung by Patsy Cline. It might have been called *I Fall to Pieces.*

As he thumbed through the Patsy Cline LPs a sudden influx of boys in cricket jumpers and girls in flowing skirts changed the climate around him. He had felt this atmosphere before. He knew what it meant. He couldn't shake this mood even as back outside and, lacking a Patsy Cline LP in a grey carrier bag he smoked another strong, continental cigarette by the Union railings.

He wanted a smart new shirt, but in the third shop he tried the assistants were staring again. He fled to a bookstore and skimmed chapters about the life and philosophy of Immanuel Kant. He became enmeshed in *The Mathematical Theory of Black Holes* by Subrahmanyan Chandrasekhar, a book he dearly wanted but couldn't afford. He read standing up for two hours. The static that had built up in his thoughts faded. It was mere nerves, he reasoned. Who wouldn't be nervous, or at least wracked with a spine-shuddering fear? The Heartbreaker was coming to his room.

Without Patsy Cline, candles or a smart new shirt he headed for home, his room that overlooked a courtyard and the backs of houses where he knew there lived other thinkers and dreamers. On the way he did, however, buy two pale green and elaborately labelled bottles of £1.99 Liebfraumilch. The board outside the newsagent shouted that Elaine Preece was still missing.

Δ

'I don't understand,' said Zara. She was pacing the room. Adrian had just moved from the bed to his chair. The sagging mattress had seemed overly charged. He still couldn't keep his feet still. He feared she'd already clocked the expression that must by now be seeping down his face. 'Why can't they track down,' she continued, 'the man who gave her the lift from the station?'

The last anyone knew of Elaine Preece was that she'd made a call from Paddington. She phoned her boyfriend, Pepper Marx, to say she'd arrived safely in London. She was supposed to be seeing an exhibition at the Tate, one that didn't interest the American. He'd even admitted that they'd had a minor tiff about it. For some reason, though, she'd rung Marx to tell him a man she'd met on the train had offered her a lift. Everyone was now obsessed with the identity of this Mr X.

'She must be with him,' said Zara. 'She's been a silly tart, we can all be a silly tart sometimes, and she's so loved-up that she doesn't realise that there's all this fuss.'

'They won't find him,' said Adrian. Everyone must surely see that Elaine had never boarded that train. The culprit was staring them in the face.

'That poor boy,' said Zara. 'He must be worried sick.'

'No Mr Marx calls his son Pepper,' said Adrian. 'Would Mr Erasmus call his son Salt? Would Mr Spinoza call his son Ketchup? There's no book called *The Condiments of Philosophy*.'

Zara paused to stare out of the window, at the houses across the courtyard. It crossed Adrian's mind that he ought to say something about the Swan King. When she turned around, though, she was trying to stifle a laugh.

'Anthony said...I mean he *lied* the other day that he knows Pepper. You know he's a rower. Pepper's only here because he's an extraordinary oarsman. Anyway Anthony says Pepper said, before the Boat Race, that he was going to "kick arse, Cambridge arse".'

'That's very gallant,' said Adrian.

'He must be going through hell.'

'Do you want some of this wine? There's a seventy-eight percent chance it's undrinkable.'

'I suppose so, if you put it like that.'

Adrian found a corkscrew in his drawer and opened a bottle. Meanwhile she crouched down by his stereo and started to flip through his LPs. The album sleeves gently tapped against one another as she ran her fingers across them. The perfect ovals of her heels lifted from her shoes as she leaned forwards. The waistband of her 501s slipped, revealing a strap of bright white skin beneath the risen hem of her green top. He could see the small of her back. He wanted to touch it. It would be like stroking part of the moon, a slender crescent moon, the soft, smiling moon he remembered from a nightlight that had glowed in his bedroom when he was a child. He ought not to tell her that he was thinking about her arse as if it were the moon.

'Adrian,' she said, swiping a tendril of hair from her face. 'You have a record called *Crumbling the Antiseptic Beauty*.' Her tone implied that he was both connoisseurishly sensitive and a pretentious twat, with a gentle stress on the twat.

'Want to hear it? It's...erm, quite fragile-sounding.'

'Lord no. Have you got anything, you know, jump-about? The Monkees?'

'I've got The Telescopes. I prefer the equipment bands to the primate bands.'

'You must have *Daydream Believer*?'

He could not say that daydreaming was no longer enough. When he'd first set eyes on her, at an introductory meeting with the tutors, he'd hidden at the back of the group while she presided at the front. She was wearing an Alice band and a Barbour jacket and a tartan miniskirt and black tights and asked lots of questions. Her voice was painfully wonderful to him. It suggested moments and evenings he would never deserve.

Until last week he had only seen her swish about here and there. Once he'd noticed her, quite by accident, pushing her bike along a cobbled street in a midmorning mist. A thick, striped scarf was wrapped around her neck and its dangling end quivered against her thigh as the stones shuddered the bike's frame.

He had spied on her once as she browsed the second-hand bookstore in the covered market. She was carrying a pineapple and a cocktail shaker and had slapped a heavy pink book down on a pile and sniggered as she walked away.

On one of his rare visits to the college bar he had watched her sitting on a bench alongside Anthony Christmas. She was laughing and joking but when Christmas tried to place his oven-glove-sized hand over hers she'd whipped it away.

Last week, when Adrian had somehow managed to sit opposite her in the Upper Reading Room he'd become so hot and distracted – the way she chewed her bottom lip as she read; the round, owlish glasses that slid up and down her nose; the cool, perfect bracelet that looked like it was made out of platinum – that he'd started to babble about how difficult she must be finding it, being stuck there with him. She'd lined up a sharpened pencil, darts player-style, and threw it straight at him. He ducked and it hit the whale-boned back of a girl in dungarees who reacted with a lot of shushing and threats.

So frightening and strange was her casual suggestion that they head out for a coffee that he almost said 'no'. Over coffee, a heated exchange occurred about whether people who wear cagoules should be banished in perpetuity or merely fined. Adrian found himself admitting that he owned two cagoules, an orange one and a green one but he preferred the toggles on the green. She must have misheard, because otherwise she wouldn't have afterwards mentioned that she might like to go for a drink later, if he was free. The sheer physical effort required to say 'yes' had half-killed him. He'd almost hyperventilated as soon as she was out of sight. But she not only turned up for the drink, she was funny and warm and didn't try to strip-mine him for tips and information like Hannah Mitchelmore. When Zara had asked why everyone saw so little of him, why, as she put it he 'cut such an obscure, no, a mysterious figure' he had not felt that she knew. He liked her – more than liked her already – *and* she didn't know.

'You've got too many small animal bands,' she said. 'Look, The Field Mice, The Sea Urchins. It's like an under-funded private zoo. I give up. You choose.'

He handed her a glass of wine. They swapped places; she was now perched on the chair as he selected an inoffensive jazz piano thing called *Train Above the City* that he hardly ever listened to. He wanted a drift in a certain direction. He wanted it to be like he had always imagined.

'Oh God,' she said. 'I can't stop thinking about how poor Pepper must be feeling. He won't rest until she comes back, and then when she comes back she's going to probably end it with him, and even if she doesn't he's never going to believe that she wasn't a silly tart, and they'll split up anyway.'

'I think,' said Adrian, without thinking, 'that we have to come to terms with the likelihood that Marx has topped her.'

'Don't say that.'

But he couldn't. It was an obvious solution to a simple problem, an Occam's Razor job and focusing on it made him feel that he wasn't talking boring crap that would make her leave in a minute.

'Think about it,' he said. 'No one remembers her at the station. No one remembers her being on the train. No one remembers seeing her at Paddington. No one saw her at the Tate. And look at him. Used to getting his own way. Far from home. Not sure of how to behave here.'

'A bit like you then?'

'Used to getting my own way?'

No, not that. Look, I don't want to think that it's him.'

She got up and started to pace again, faster than the plodding rhythms of the music, the now-empty glass resting against her hip.

'I'm sorry,' said Adrian, 'I shouldn't have said that.'

'I can't help thinking that if she's gone, and I don't want to think that she's gone, but if she is, that it can happen just like that. Like that. Out of the blue. So suddenly, without any sort of warning at all. And that could happen to me. I could be next.'

He forced a smile he hoped would appear sympathetic and caring. His hands were trembling.

'It hasn't happened,' he said, 'and sweetheart, it's so unusual, so random. And it hasn't happened yet. No one really knows anything.'

It was as equally random, he will later conclude, that here he somehow managed to say the right thing.

'Can I have a hug?' she said. She took a step towards him but turned her head to the window as she reached out to put her glass alongside his. She paused, half-stooped, blinking at something outside. 'Who on earth is that?'

The man across the courtyard had never frightened him, not in the slightest, not even at the start. When Adrian had chosen this house in backstreets where a fog often hung that shunned the rest of the city; where the chugging machinery of an all-night bakery provided an atonal soundtrack for night-walks and moon-gazing; where the Victorian terraces were famous for their shoddy masonry and for being where the children were murdered in *Jude the Obscure*, he had done so to live among strangers. His fellow lodgers came from all over and were not a clique or a gang of friends from college. He had needed assurance that his new housemates could not know. If they did know, he would never get anything done. This had been the problem in his first year, when he had lived in college.

On the day he moved in he found a yellow Post-It stuck to the sagging mattress. There was a note in red felt-tip.

WATCH OUT FOR THE SWAN KING!!!

It hadn't taken long for The Swan King to make his presence felt. Out the back, beyond the brick courtyard where the other residents dried their washing and left their bikes and smoked joints and cigarettes on the step, over in the house opposite, at a bedroom window that aligned perfectly with Adrian's, every evening, as daylight faded The Swan King appeared.

The Swan King's room was stark and bare. Adrian could see no shelves or furniture. A naked light bulb fired the Swan King's outline with a dazzle so white it became a charcoal-grey halo around his head and shoulders. He was tall, lean, bony, his face clearly long and angular, even though both the distance and the glare smudged his features and made his age impossible to guess. Adrian understood why the room's previous occupant had described a swan and a king. The man across the courtyard looked like a grand and imperious swan.

Every night the Swan King sat at that window. He did not move. He did not smoke. He did not scratch or shift his position. He did not pick up a mug or a glass to take a sip of something. He did not write or read. He stared. When Adrian studied late into the night he could look up from his desk and The Swan King would always be watching. In the morning, The Swan King would be gone. At dusk, he would return. Adrian had waved a few times. The Swan King never waved back.

'Yikes, lordy!' Zara stepped away from the window and wrapped her arms around her chest. 'Who's that?'

'I don't know,' said Adrian.

'What's he doing?'

'Looking.'

'Doesn't that give you the creeps?'

'I never get up to anything.'

'Adrian, I do not believe, not for one minute, that you don't get up to anything.'

'I've got used to him. He's just some local eccentric.'

'Weirdo, you mean.'

'He's called the Swan King.'

'That's cute. And you don't just sit in here listening to The Badgers, do you?' She tapped her temple. 'There's always an excruciating amount going on in there. Anyway, I was about to get a hug.'

Her eyes were bright blue planets now, planets from the outer solar system, but close to him, brilliant, hazy.

'Shut the curtains,' she said. 'He doesn't have to know everything.'

Afterwards they lay in the gorge their bodies made in the sagging mattress. Moonlight scanned them from the tiniest of gaps in the curtains. His stomach was pressed into the warmth of her back. He could hear her breathing and smell an apple-scented shampoo that lingered on her hair. He was calculating the probabilities that led to his arrival here. This situation had not developed before, with the girl from home, the one he should never think about. He predicted that he was going to have to maintain a stiff upper lip. Zara was sure to say something pretty soon, when she realised her mistake. He was going to have to be controlled.

'Zara,' he said. 'You OK?'

'Do you know what?' she said. 'Anthony got me back to his room once, and he'd put out all these tatty candles, and sprayed all these rose petals that clearly came out of a packet on his duvet, and then he put on this old scratchy record, and then he gave me a glass of tepid champagne. The cheap stuff, you know, and the glass looked like the sort that you get given free at a petrol station. He'd left a packet of green condoms on his dresser. He'd even put them on a napkin.'

'You didn't, did you?'

'Adrian. He plays lacrosse, remember.'

He wanted to tell her that earlier he'd had all these plans for tonight but had not been able to conclude them. Now this had happened. It had happened because it was meant to be. The Universe had intervened to help him today. Maybe there was magic after all.

'Zara,' said Adrian, brushing her hair away from her ear so he could whisper into it. 'What do Anthony and Hugo Christmas call their dad?'

'Shut your trap and go to sleep.'

He let his head sink into the pillow and squeezed her tighter to him. He wanted to get up, put on The Monkees and dance around. He didn't know how to dance, though, and he wasn't wearing any clothes. She would surely run away then.

'Why are you laughing?' she muttered.

He couldn't tell her. He couldn't tell her that he overpoweringly felt as if he had equalized. There had been all that defeat before he came here. One-nil, two-nil, ten-nil down. She had wiped it all out. No one would remember now. No one would know.

'Poor Pepper,' said Zara, 'I hope he's OK. I hope he's not suffering. I hope she comes back tomorrow. I think that would just cheer everybody up. It would, wouldn't it? Everything would seem alright again. Normal. If she came back, Adrian?'

He was falling asleep. He would later suspect that the last thing he'd said to her must have been, 'I expect Elaine's living with the Swan King now.'

Δ

The next night they returned to the room before the pubs had shut. She tossed her shoulder bag onto the bed. She undid the band that tied up her hair, something that she would not be doing if she did not intend to stay. For a moment back there, it had been touch and go. He thought he'd lost her already. Quickly and stupidly.

'I was only joking,' he said.

'It wouldn't have sounded like a joke to him,' she said. 'He's an excruciating idiot but he's not a moron.'

She smirked. He felt forgiven, that he'd squeaked it. It was a warning, though, an omen. Now in front of the window again, she propped up her chin with her fist, like she was studying a weird and beguiling portrait.

'He's out again,' she said. 'Watching us. I don't like him.' She thrust her hands into her sides and poked out her tongue.

Adrian moved and sat behind her on the end of the bed. She took up half of the window, standing there in her short crimson dress, the backs of her knees taut. To the left of her ear the Swan King hung in his box of white dazzle. Adrian fought a desire to wrap his arms around her waist and drag her back onto the bed. Such a tactic seemed a bit rugby-player to him, too hearty, too Anthony Christmas. It had been the most fantastic and unexpected day until Christmas had almost ruined it.

That morning he'd awoken with the summer's heat packed around the pair of them. Zara hadn't resisted when he slid his palms across her thighs and shoulders and waist. They lay there for an hour, the soles of her feet pressing down on his shins. She did not say that she must leave. After she'd eased herself out of bed, as she pulled on her jeans, she did not look at him with horror. She shook her head in front of his mirror and said, 'Oh God, look at me. Tina Turner hair.' She stole one of his French cigarettes and smoked it at the window. 'The King is dead,' she said. 'Let's go for breakfast.'

In a narrow, whitewash-and-Formica café they ate fry-ups washed down with orange juice and frothy coffees. She told him that her father was the Duke of Catford and then laughed at how long it took him to twig. He toyed with lying about who he was as she explained her Huguenot heritage. Her family had outposts in Berlin and Holland and a fortune built on lace making, then the mass-manufacture of padlocks and now property, land and investments. She told him that this weather felt mild to her. Until she was fourteen she'd spent every summer on her uncle's estate on Mustique. His name was Xavier Dupleix.

'He plays lacrosse,' she said.

She held Adrian's hand under the table when she said this, then suggested that as the day was already useless for anything other than foolish decadence they should go for a picnic down by the riverbank, somewhere shady and secluded. It would be like in a film, a French film starring English people. They could call themselves the *Sacerdotes*, the Sun Worshippers.

Soon he was sitting on her bed, on a mattress that didn't sag, in a spacious oblong room that looked out onto cedar trees and a croquet lawn. She rummaged in her wardrobe and threw clothes and blankets over her shoulder. He narrowly missed being hit by a picnic basket when he moved to switch on the portable television. The one o'clock news was on. Elaine Preece was still the headline story.

Zara stopped chucking things out of her wardrobe and budged him up with her thigh. She leant forwards at the screen, chewing her forefinger as the newsreader said that concerns were mounting for the safety of Oxford University student Elaine Preece who had now been missing for six days. A policewoman read a statement at a press conference. There would be a reconstruction of the last known movements of Elaine Preece tomorrow. Behind her sat the family, a mother and father and two older brothers, plus at the end of the table the giant, rocky outcrop Pepper Marx.

'That poor boy,' said Zara. 'That poor, poor dear.'

Elaine's mother got up and read from a piece of paper she could hardly keep still. Her voice strained and faltered.

'Elaine is kind and loving and vivacious and she has her whole life ahead of her, so if you know anything, if you think you have seen her, or if you think you are looking after her, please, please let the police know.'

She was led away by her sons and Pepper Marx.

Back in the newsroom, a phone number was displayed for anyone with information.

'Why have they announced that?' said Adrian. 'It's clearly him. He interns for some Republican senator who flogs arms to death squads in Nicaragua.'

'And that makes him a murderer, does it?' said Zara.

'Sort of, yes.'

She placed her hands over her face. He put his arm around her shoulders and squeezed her.

'I'm sorry,' he said. 'That was thoughtless. Shall we go out? Get some sun?'

She shrugged him off and made a circuit of the room, not looking at him but at the corners of the room one by one until she came back to the end of the bed and grabbed hold of the tartan blanket she'd tossed there earlier. She took one of its edges in each of her hands and stared down at him, her eyes glistening. 'We can't go out,' she said. 'Not now.'

He girded himself. He must not stagger away like a dog with three legs. She raised her arms and spread the blanket across her shoulders. She collapsed onto him, pulling the blanket over their heads. She forced her tongue into his mouth. It felt strong and it felt alive.

Later, in some cavernous bar, a deconsecrated church now called Augustus, he had felt almost as if he was looking down on the tops of their heads and the bottle of Sauvignon Blanc that sat between them on the table. She hadn't mentioned Elaine since the appeal on the news. Elaine had doubly vanished. The Heartbreaker was kissing him and Elaine was gone, but why then did she suddenly stop kissing? Who was this sharking towards their table, a tall figure in a blazer and chinos and wearing cufflinks on a weeknight? Anthony Christmas paused in front of their table, hanging his thumb from his belt buckle. He smirked, like he was baffled when he realized who she was with. He spoke down to Adrian as if Adrian were some peasant transposed from the Middle Ages to point at electric lights and mechanical timepieces. Christmas asked a number of dumb questions. He made his voice slow on purpose. Like all the others, he knew. And because he knew, because this particular one knew, Adrian had let his black cat out of its black bag.

Zara had now sat beside him on the end of the bed. They were looking at the Swan King. They had not spoken for some time. This did not seem strained or difficult.

'What are you thinking?' she said. 'Something excruciating, I expect.'

He was reimagining all the things that she had done to him that afternoon. Remembering her lips and thighs helped dissolve the ball of stress that pulsed in his abdomen. He tried to convince himself that no one really knew. He tried not to think about what he'd ranted at Anthony Christmas. Zara would only give him a *Get Out of Jail Free* card the once.

'I'm thinking about the Swan King,' he said.

'He's a freaky voyeur,' said Zara. 'By night he keeps an eye on you, but by day he goes rampaging around the gardens, stealing knickers and dog blankets.'

'Dog blankets?'

'He has weird tastes.'

'He's probably like Beethoven, or Wittgenstein.'

'He plays lacrosse.'

'He's probably working out a knotty problem.'

'Look, he's just staring. He hasn't moved.' Zara knelt up on the bed and wrapped her arms around Adrian's neck. 'See, he didn't even blink when I did that.'

'If he did react, you'd have a kitten.'

'He's looking, though, he's filthy.'

'He was looking before I moved here.'

'Take me to a hotel, Adrian. I can't be doing with this.'

She dropped off the bed and pulled the curtains. The room seemed quieter as well as darker.

'I want to know what he's doing,' said Zara.

'Write him a fan letter.'

'Let's play Knock Down Ginger.'

'I think he's just...you know...quiet. I don't like the idea of disturbing anyone.'

'That's not the impression you gave earlier. Anthony doesn't know what a feudalist is. He probably thinks it's a judo move.'

'I said I'm sorry about that.'

'Tomorrow night,' said Zara. 'Let's go and find that house. I want to see the whites of his eyes. I want to know if he really is a pervert.'

Δ

The next night followed a shimmering, heat-haze morning and blistering afternoon. The city became the set of the film adaptation of a long lost Edwardian novel, the story of the final family gathering before the outbreak of war, or the engagement party of a socially mismatched couple: *The Looking-Glass Party, To the Swanhouse*. Adrian was assembling a cast and situations, storing up ideas that he hoped would charm Zara later. Concerned, he wanted to distract her from the true crime drama they'd watched earlier.

In the midday swelter, they had waited at the station, part of a crowd it was hoped would have their memories jogged by a policewoman dressed in jeans like Elaine Preece's jeans and an England rugby top like the one she had worn on the day that she vanished, wearing a cox cap like hers and carrying a bag identical to the one she'd taken with her to London. Pepper Marx, lumbering, solemn, had walked this doppelganger up the station steps and onto the concourse. The rest of the reconstruction was shown on the six o'clock news. Adrian had watched it on Zara's portable. The footage of Pepper Mark and the Ghost-Elaine canoodling and kissing on a metal bench had Zara in tears again.

'She's supposed to be able to drink a yard of ale before cooking a three-course meal for a six-man crew,' Adrian had said, 'including an onion soup starter and crudités.' He'd read this in *The Daily Star*, in an account of her other foibles and an index of her Pre-Marx conquests. 'She doesn't sound daft enough to wander off with some Norman Bates job.' He was going to add that she was obviously daft enough to go out with Psycho-Killer Qu'est-ce que c'est, but for once caught himself in time. He was learning. You could say anything if you were strong, nothing if you were weak.

'You said,' Zara replied, 'you said that she never left. You said she was living with the Swan King.'

'I didn't,' he said. 'I didn't say that.'

'Well, someone out there has done something to her.'

He'd tried his best to sidetrack her into staying in her room but this time she was stubborn and passionless. Now he was following her along a terraced street as she nodded at each of the houses they passed. It was still humid. A grey mist swirled around the streetlamps, glistened on brickwork, smothered the stairwells that led down to basement flats. That chugging bass line, the machinery of the all-night bakery droned in the distance, sometimes a faint hum, but then so loud that it sounded like something was padding across the paving slabs behind them.

She was counting down the houses. Last night she had stood at his window and guesstimated the number of houses to the Swan King's. She stopped and turned to him.

'I think it's this one,' she said.

The house was a three-storey Victorian affair with white window boxes and steps leading up to a black door with a wrought-iron knocker.

A dash of moonlight glimmered on the pane of the highest dormer window. There were no lights on inside. It was thick with dark in there. Adrian knew that it did align with his house, but he wasn't going to confirm this.

'I don't think it is,' he said. 'Let's go. We can have a beer somewhere, OK?'

'Stop faffing, Adrian, this is it.'

She planted one of her deck shoes on the lowest step of the Swan King's house. What little breeze there was blew her hair across her eyes. Adrian could not quite read her expression.

'OK,' she said, and bounded up the steps. It was probably going to be a lot worse for him if he didn't stand shoulder-to-shoulder with her.

On the top step, in front of the door now, he looked up. The triangular point of the roof seemed to narrow and stretch until it merged with the night sky. He put his arm around Zara's waist, loosely, supportively, to hide any suggestion he was thinking about anything else. He was, though: the room and the bed and the journey to morning. She took hold of the doorknocker between her finger and thumb. The tendons in her wrist flexed as she slammed it into the ironwork panel.

A metallic bang reverberated around the houses.

They waited. It was hard to imagine how they could hear any footsteps or movement from behind the thickness of that door. She hit it again, harder now. This time a tone buzzed in the air that after a few seconds faded into the hum of the bakery. She flicked her eyes leftwards at Adrian. Her fingers intermingled with his fingers. She raised both their hands. Together they grabbed hold of the knocker and crashed it into the panel as hard as they could.

A shout came from behind them. Lights in several opposing houses had flashed in upper story rooms.

'I've had enough,' said Adrian, 'we're going to get lynched.' He tried to tug her back down the steps. She resisted, but unbalanced, managed only one more limp and weedier tap on the door before she followed him. He threw his arm around her shoulder and pulled her head alongside his own so it rested on his shoulder and he quickened his stride, their stride, forcing them along until they were at the corner and out of earshot.

Δ

Back in his room she slumped on his bed, her head cradled in her hands, her hair breeze-blown into wild tufts. She was staring at him as if he'd done something. He'd been stared at like this before. He tried not to think about that stare: the girl, the reservoir, the visit. His thighs wouldn't stop itching and he couldn't stop scratching them and tapping his feet, not the image he wanted to project, and he was gawping at Zara, ogling, drowning in her.

He tried to remember the situations from the Edwardian film he'd concocted earlier, the one that would have characters called Zara and Adrian, who could escape all this war and stigma and travel by steamer to Egypt, where he would build dams and railroads and she would have itches she couldn't scratch on verandas and terraces.

'I was going to buy you some wine,' he said, 'but I forgot, and I was going to get a cassette of The Monkees...'

'Adrian, please, I'm thinking.' This didn't sound good. She got up and opened the curtains. 'Fucking hell,' she said.

Out across the courtyard, the Swan King was suspended in his oblong of light.

'He might be deaf,' said Adrian. 'We could've banged all night...'

'What if she's in there?'

'She's not.'

'What if she's there and we didn't do anything?'

'We just did. It was pointless, but we did something.'

'And now he knows the net is closing in, now he knows that we know, that I know...and you said she was living with the Swan King.'

She was standing rigidly erect now, her arms at her sides, and for a moment he could see a much older Zara, a woman in wig and gown, addressing a judge; a woman at a lectern, reading out a report to a committee; a woman at the head of a boardroom table, shoulder-padded-up and regally out-performing all the dumb rich men.

'Zara, I'd just like to have a nice time now and forget about everything.'

'It's him. I know it.'

'It's Pepper Marx.'

Her barrister pose vanished. She started to shake a little.

'You only say that, because...it's like the thing with Anthony.'

'And I could say, sweetheart, that you only think it's that poor bastard over there because you can't work out what dynasty he belongs to.'

'You *want* it to be Pepper.'

'Do you love him or something?'

She picked a jotter from his desk and threw it at him. He raised his forearms to deflect it.

'I've never met either of them, for God's sake.'

She grimaced. He cringed. More than cringed, he was flooded by a terrible awareness. He'd felt like this before, after the visit to his parents' house and then, afterwards, when slowly, methodically, street-by-street, house-to-house, everybody knew.

'I thought she's your friend?' he said.

'I don't know her, OK? Might have seen her once, that's all.'

She dipped her head and her eyes receded into a shadowy band beneath her fringe. Her upright posture collapsed, as if the case had been dismissed. She shuffled towards him on the balls of her feet.

'We're going to do something,' she whispered. 'We're going to watch him back until he comes to us.'

Adrian made some coffee. He found an ashtray. He stole a chair from the kitchen; a rickety back-breaker that he had to sit on because Zara complained it was shitty. He turned off the light. They pulled the chairs together and sat thigh-to-thigh. The grey mist made the Swan King seem even less distinct, smoother, almost featureless. Adrian lit up and blew smoke against the pane, blocking out the Swan King for an instant. This was all stupid. In an hour, tops, Zara would either get bored rigid or fall asleep.

She didn't say anything. She watched. It couldn't be any worse if he'd found himself madly in love with a girl into birdwatching or golf or Formula One. The Swan King stared back at them, or through them. That house was empty, Adrian suspected, the rooms bare and gaping. It crossed his mind, though, that if all he assumed about the Swan King were correct, then maybe what they were doing now would turn out for the best. Zara would be purged of this irrational conviction that the Swan King had something to do with Elaine Preece. Tonight's adventure might steer Zara past this emotional tourist trap about Elaine Preece, who it turned out she didn't even know, who she had perhaps seen once out of the corner of her eye, a bobbed hairstyle in a queue at some ball or boatclub disco. Everyone was so wrapped up in being part of this great drama: Zara and Hannah and Gareth and Anthony Christmas and the whole student body and the rest of the country and the media. Tourists and twitchers, the lot of them. They wanted to belong to this. They needed to be significant. To be witnesses. This would destroy them. He himself would not be destroyed, not now, now that he had found a Zara, now that they were together.

He found himself thinking back to the time before the visit to his parents' house, before the shockwave, and how this, to be sitting here with someone like her would have seemed the most magical situation possible. For the first time, he knew. She was not going to realise. She was not going to leave him.

They sat there, hand-in-hand, staring at the Swan King. An hour passed, then half another.

'Adrian?' said Zara.

'Ah, she's still alive. Thought I'd lost you.'

'Can I ask you something? Why doesn't he bother you?'

'Worse things happen.'

'I would be scared. I am scared. It concerns me that you're not scared.'

'If I saw him somewhere else. If I thought he had some interest in me, or in you, then I'd be scared.'

'Look at him, though. He knows we're looking and he's done nothing to…I don't know…he's not even made sure that we're not bothered.'

'He's probably thinking about string theory or the transit of Pluto.'

'It's too weird.'

'Look.' Adrian leant back on the rest of his chair, forcing her to turn to him and away from the Swan King. 'The thing is, when I look at him, or when I know he's there…I've always thought, well, I've assumed that I'll end up like that. You know. On my own. In my head. Empty house.'

She frowned. She squeezed his hand. This was good. She was coming back to him.

'That's dumb,' she said. 'You need to have more confidence in yourself.'

'Look, I should say…I should say that that's how I felt until now, get me?'

'Adrian, honey, you're smart and witty and…well, you're odd but in a nice way. You're a bit of a nightmare, but in a nice way. You're very honest, but that's not always…I don't know. You'll be fine, Adrian.

Believe me. You just need to get out more. Spend more time with people.'

He felt flushed. His ribs and the bones in his arms seemed to heat up. He imagined that the Swan King across the way would see a red flare bloom in the quiet kid's room.

His only frame of reference was a moment at the reservoir, four years ago now. When he'd reached the edge of the copse, no longer able to keep his distance so easily after he'd tracked the girl called Susannah all along the path she always took in the mornings. He was peering around the trunk of an oak tree. Wood pigeons called and underbrush crackled behind him. Ahead, sunlight prickled on the surface of the water. There were no anglers that day or windsurfers. Only the two of them. She in her damson-coloured velour tracksuit top, her black headband and her headphones, her Walkman strapped to her waist, jiggling as she adopted an 'I'm a little teapot short and stout' pose. She swivelled on her hips, her hair swinging, her breasts moving beneath her top and he was hot then too, flushed, his bones overheating, only the two of them.

Zara fell forward onto the desk. Her hair fell over her eyes and she wedged the heels of her hands into her forehead.

'You're getting knackered, baby, aren't you?' said Adrian. 'Do you want to go to bed?'

'Oh Christ,' she said. 'I wish I could be like you. I wish I could be so cool.'

'C'mon, you're the coolest person I know.'

'People think that, but I'm not.'

'I think you're letting everything get to you. Look at him, out there, wasting his life away. We should get some sleep. I used to go to the lab before I met you.'

She lifted her head and craned her neck, poking it forwards and stared hard at the Swan King, as if willing him to rise and float over the courtyard towards them.

'I hate myself,' she said.

'I don't want to hear you say that again,' said Adrian. 'And now, you know now there's us, I want you to stop me saying things like that, too, OK?'

'You don't understand.'

She hunched up. She kept still for some time, with Adrian circling his palm around her shoulder blades. The Swan King stayed where he was, passive, motionless, dreaming whatever dreams prevented him from sleeping.

Adrian's eyes started to feel crusty and sore. She may well have fallen asleep beside him now. Maybe he could ease her onto the bed. She would hardly notice that she was being moved. In the morning she would feel better. Maybe in the morning Elaine would be found and this would end. He and Zara could finish their stupid degrees and swim off together. He even hoped she would start snoring so he would have something to tease her about tomorrow.

When the night sky outside started to lighten above the roofs and the odd bird started to sing, Zara slowly sat up and without saying anything reached out for the cigarette packet. She lit up, took a deep drag and then passed him the cigarette.

'Can I tell you something?' she said. 'Can I tell you something I've never told anyone before?'

'Of course.' He blinked his eyes open, his pulse now throbbing powerfully at his temples.

'Have you ever been to Mustique?'

'I went to Calais once. On a school trip. It was shit. I mean, really shit.'

'It's a beautiful place. We used to go every year. Stay with my uncle. He's got a villa. He's got a villa on Mustique. When I was twelve I started to go on my own. My sister was very ill when I was little. She has a hole in her heart. She couldn't travel. They wouldn't leave her. So I had these big adventures. Grown-up little me. Jet-set Cindy. I used to wear these little red sunglasses.'

The villa. She'd only visited there alone three times, she said, but now it felt as if she always lived on the island. School and London were just snippets of dreams she'd had there. The parties. The heat. Swimming pools and boat trips. Snorkelling with an Israeli girl with a thick, incomprehensible accent. Birds of paradise. Lizards and geckos. Ice. Uncle Xav.

'Sounds like a Lilt advert,' said Adrian. Zara became emotional, shaky. He didn't know what to say. The Swan King stared back at them. She continued.

She had kind of known it was going on the first time she was there on her own. She wasn't stupid. She knew that he shouldn't be giving her all that rum and Coke; that they shouldn't really be swimming in the pool late at night while Aunt Sabrina and everyone else was asleep. But there was something naughty about it, something fun. When she was thirteen, yes, she definitely knew that it was wrong that she would wake to find him sitting on the end of her bed, part-lit up in a slant of moonbeam, cradling a long tall glass. He would clatter the ice around the depths of the glass. He would tell her jokes that she was still too young to understand. He would put his hand over her mouth so no one could hear her laugh. He would kiss her goodnight. But he would leave. He would not be there in the morning.

The last time, though, the last time that she went there, she knew she shouldn't have let him put his hands around her waist on the jetty. She shouldn't have kissed him back when he'd kissed her. She certainly shouldn't have given him that look as she'd left the party downstairs and traipsed off to bed, drowsy now, and drunk and feeling radiantly triumphant for brushing off the ugly boy from Miami. If the Belgian couple hadn't argued so furiously on the landing outside her room while Uncle Xavier knelt beside her bed and stroked her hair, anything could have happened. Something would have happened, for sure.

Adrian listened with a mounting sense of rage and helplessness. He had not believed that this sort of thing really happened. Rumours and accusations like these were made up by tabloids to make people angry, to make people scared, just like they made up that Elaine Preece drank a yard of ale a night and had taken sixteen lovers in the year before Pepper Marx. He felt young, a baby, weak despite a straining tension in his arms and fists. He wanted to have been there, on the island, to stand sentinel, her watchdog, her guardsman. She needed protecting. She would need protecting forever.

'The thing is,' she said. 'The thing is. I did want it to happen. I was disappointed.'

'C'mon, honey,' he said. 'You were just a little girl.'

'Six years ago.' She fluttered her arm across her torso. 'I'm not really a little girl, am I?'

'But he did it.'

'He did it.' She turned to the window. 'Oh God, oh no.'

The light across the courtyard had vanished. The window was black, the interior invisible.

'I don't believe it,' said Adrian.

'Bastard moved. Bastard, bastard, bastard.'

'He must have fucked off while we weren't looking.'

'Bastard.'

'Well, I can't believe he did it to spite us.'

'I'm going round. I know she's there.'

Zara stood up, her face ash-blue in the half-light, her hair matted and glinting.

'Are you going to let him get away with it?' she said.

'Who?'

'Don't look at me like that.'

'Listen. You ever feel that something you did was someone else doing it?'

'I want to have a bath.'

'You understand me. I think you know me, but not in the way the others know me. I need to tell you something, before we fall asleep, before this thing passes.'

It was so bright outside now that it could be any time of day. They lay beside each other on the bed. He smoked three whole cigarettes stub-to-stub before he'd dismissed all the wrong places to start.

Δ

In the Café Metz they played *Hand on Your Heart* by Kylie Minogue, then *Sealed with a Kiss* by Jason Donovan but Adrian wasn't even a little bit sick. He liked these songs now. They were orange and yellow, bright and joyous, like Christmas carols. He conceded that he would have to apologize to Anthony Christmas. Any friend of Zara's was a friend of his. He was waiting for Zara. Zara was late.

The shutters were open and tables and chairs were set out on the pavement. Adrian was inside, in the shade, sitting beneath a framed Jacques Brel poster and half way through his second beer. Outside, in what he usually referred to as Little Pretentious Street boys in cricket whites and girls in loose pastel skirts crossed the front of the cafe and the usually annoying poet on the corner tried to stop each and every one of them with his hand-pressed pamphlets. Women who glided their pushchairs past the tables made Adrian smile. Zara would be here soon.

On the other side of the café, below the room-length mirror, a kid in an indigo tie-dyed T-shirt was explaining to a girl with spiky hair that

Gazza is a fat Geordie bastard who was lucky to score that goal against Albania. She was wearing Ray-Bans and looked like she would listen to *Disintegration* by The Cure in bed. She probably slept in black sheets and owned a sprawling, proliferating collection of black underwear. They were playing footsie under the table, just like Zara had in Augustus.

Down the aisle a woman in a peasant-style headscarf cut up a baguette saucisson that her four tiny children set upon like squeaking seagulls. Next to them a lithe, middle-aged man with viciously parted and slicked-down hair was reading *The Mathematical Theory of Black Holes*. The idea of the book now seemed dry and inessential to Adrian. There was no longer a need to hide in maths and entropy. He scanned the room and sipped his beer. None of them knew, not the footsie-players or the headscarf lady or the black hole theorist. The mothers in the street did not know. The poet on the corner did not know. Kylie and Jason and Gazza did not know. No one knew, except Zara. The Swan King had done this. The Swan King brought them together.

He reconfigured the events of the last week in patterns and sequences without the Swan King. What if there was no Swan King? What if Zara hadn't been so confused and terrified of the Swan King? What if Zara had not misread the Swan King? What if Elaine Preece had not gone missing? What if they'd spent their evenings in her room, not his? What if, on that first night she'd come round to drink wine and listen to records the Swan King had spooked her sufficiently that she'd made her excuses and left? What if on that first night she came to his room he had lit candles and played Patsy Cline or *Crumbling the Antiseptic Beauty*? What if, when they knocked on the Swan King's door the Swan King had appeared and shyly given a plausible explanation for his behaviour, or agreed to stop it? What if no Swan King existed?

Without the Swan King Factor it was extremely unlikely that they would have reached this point, that they would have been honest with one another, that they could have come to this profound understanding. He would not have found himself drinking beer in the afternoon. He would not be tempted to go and buy one of the corner-poet's pamphlets. He would not be anticipating her arrival in every shadow in the doorway, each gentle footfall or the shimmer of a dress.

A girl in a dress shimmered into the Café Metz. It was not Zara but a brunette with crinkle-cut hair. Adrian realized that he was going to have to get used to how long it can take girls to get ready. That morning he and Zara had woken up close to noon. She'd said that she would meet him here. First, she was going to go back to her room and have a bath and get changed. He imagined her lying in the bath, bubbles and suds swirling like clouds across her midriff, her hair wet and balled-up at her nape, staring at the ceiling, realizing herself what had happened, how she was free, how they were both now free. He pictured her powdering her body and drying her hair and slipping on a dress, maybe the crimson one that she knew he liked so much. He imagined that she was nearly here, striding, majestic, her bag slung at hip. Maybe, though, she'd inadvertently dropped off to sleep and would wake up soon in a panic of concern, fretting that he was angry with her, hoping he was OK. He was going to have to get used to this, to Zara being late.

The girl with the crinkle-cut hair was standing on one leg in front of the man reading about black holes. She was scratching one calf with the uppers of her other sandal. He stood up and they kissed each other on both cheeks as if they were in Barcelona or something.

'Have you heard?' she said.

He frowned and shook his head.

Adrian downed the dregs of his beer. There was only a year left in this film-set. There was only a year to go hemmed in by ramparts and quadrangles. Now that he had met Zara he could enjoy this last year. He would be unafraid. There would be holidays and weekends and evenings under bunting and Chinese lanterns. He would meet many new people and look them in the eye. He would become one of them. He would get his stupid Physics and Philosophy degree out of the way and she would graduate in PPE and afterwards they would live and marry and earn.

The girl with crinkle-cut hair said, 'It's terrible, isn't it?'

It hadn't been terrible last night. Adrian had never talked about it before, at least not like he'd talked last night, not even to the psychiatrist. He'd never explained what had happened at the reservoir. He'd said her name out loud for the first time in years. He whispered it to himself now, then held it in the back of his mouth like a cough sweet as he ordered another drink from the waitress.

He'd been sixteen. It was spring. Everything was damp and waiting. His mother mentioned that someone new had moved in next door. This didn't bother him until his parents threw one of their parties, their quarterly shindigs that always ended with his mum plonked on the living room table bellowing *Anyone Who Had a Heart* into a bottle of Malibu, and his dad's mate Derek 'Killjoy' Killick squaring up to someone who looked a bit like the bloke who might have shagged his Petra when he was on the rig back in '77. Adrian usually stayed upstairs, or over at a friend's when there was a party, but no one was around that weekend. In any case he was generally feeling more sociable, talkative and grown-up and there really wasn't much else to do other than drift around his own house, watching the neighbours cackle and drink until he'd first caught sight of her.

Susannah.

Susannah in profile as viewed from the telephone chair in the hall. Leaning against the fridge, cradling a wineglass, saying something to Mum's extremely tall friend Little Viv.

Her floral dress and fading denim jacket.

The scarlet lips and cascade of wavy hair.

The goldish glitter around her eyes that he noticed as he passed and couldn't help focusing on as he hovered in the kitchen and tried to find something to say.

Watching her marooned on the end of the black leather sofa, her fingers caressing Bombay Mix in a Tupperware bowl as Colin and Mandy Teakle went on and on about time-shares in that consonant-free language of theirs.

Following her from room to room.

The brown lights. The brown surfaces.

That creeping sensation.

Making a shivery attempt to talk to her but Susannah not hearing and heading for the bathroom.

Then she was gone.

He lay upstairs on his bed, unable to sleep. Down below they were playing Phil Collins's *Sussudio* over and over again.

A strange urgency overtook the next few weeks. He started to contrive ways of meeting her. He would sit cross-legged on the green with his homework after school and watch her house. He was continually volunteering to put the rubbish out so he could linger in the front garden for as long as possible. He exhausted the dog on long walks that were actually repeated circuits of the green and the back alley where he hoped he might run into her as if by chance. He filled in dozens and dozens of coupons and questionnaires and wrote letters to the *Melody Maker* slagging off Simple Minds and joined book clubs so he could keep sauntering off to the letterbox just in case she happened to be posting something when he was there. He was out of the house so frequently that his mother thought he'd started smoking and his dad gave him a right talking-to.

Late at night he would lie in bed and through the cork walls hear her playing Terence Trent D'Arby next door. He would drown in his bed imagining a beach hut and pale silver sand dunes and her glitter-eyes and wine-bottle shoulders as she shrugged off her denim jacket and unbuttoned her dress, opening its wings in front of him. He'd told Zara last night that it was only now that he realized that this happens to everyone in some way at some time but then, way out on his own, he was lost in an outer, elliptical orbit, floating with comets and space dust, an astronaut looking down on the strips of green land between the cul-de-sacs and no through roads.

If he stood by his bedroom window with the curtains pulled he could squint through the crack and watch her squat thrusting or skipping on the patio next-door, svelte and muscular in pistachio green Lycra. In the summer, during the weekend afternoons she would sunbathe on the lawn in a zebra-print bikini, her thighs parted and the line where her breasts met tightening and relaxing as she turned the pages of chunky soft-backed books. She looked to him like one of the younger members of the cast of a Sunday night TV drama, the sort Dad's newspaper complained about. A girl whose family ran a boat yard. A very pretty girl who couldn't help falling in love with the other crewmembers of a cross-channel ferry. By the late summer he'd only heard her say his name once, in passing as she breezed by him outside Our Price: 'Hi, Ade.' By now he'd worked out that most mornings she left the house early to jog. He immediately embarked on a new physical fitness regime. He would rise early and put on tracksuit bottoms and then wait at the door until he heard her door open and shut. He'd count down a minute before he followed. She always jogged to the reservoir.

Adrian's spine stiffened so abruptly that he cracked the back of his head on the Jacques Brel poster. He remembered how Zara had just listened when he'd explained this last night. She'd squeezed his hand. She nuzzled against him as if it didn't matter. That's when it lifted, all their knowing. Across the way, the black holes man was holding both the hands of the girl with the crinkle-cut hair.

'It can only be a matter of time now,' she said.

'Have they released any details?' he said.

Adrian squeaked his finger around the rim of his glass. He hadn't done what they all said he had done. Even *she* hadn't said that he was doing what they later said he was doing, at least not to his face, not to his parents. The day after the reservoir she'd showed up at home. He was upstairs, lolling on his bed, reading. Since she shouted at him at the reservoir he'd done nothing but read. Diagrams and equations seemed to block it out. If he concentrated for long enough on clean lines and definites the reservoir would soon fade. It would be as if it had never happened. He heard his mum being friendly in the hall. His Mum said, 'Ooh hello, Su.' Their heels clicked along the hall and into the kitchen. About ten minutes later, dad bellowed up the stairs.

In the kitchen, the coffee percolator had been left to gabble. Grains spiralled in the jug. Susannah, in lilac gym top and black leggings had edged herself into the corner between the fridge and the sink. His Mum was leaning against the breakfast bar, her hands pressed on the edges, her knuckles white. Skinny and sprung, his dad looked like the bizarre copulation of a Peperami and a Swan Vesta.

'This is a mistake, right, Ade?'

Adrian couldn't say anything. He just stared at his dad. Something flashed then fell from his dad's face. He turned, walked out of the backdoor and slammed it. Adrian wanted to run. He couldn't look Susannah or his mum in the eyes and found himself staring at a wall-mounted cabinet of wineglasses and brandy balloons. Fangs of light shone on their curves.

'Adrian,' said Susannah, her voice level and sharp. 'Look, you must be at that age where you're getting urges and that. We all remember what it's like, don't we?' She nodded at mum, who nodded back but Susannah was smiling as she spoke, like she was enjoying this, as if despite what she was saying she was relishing this, not what he had done, that much was clear, but what she was able to say now. 'You can't follow girls around. You've got to keep your thoughts, and all the other things to yourself. I'm sorry I've had to come round like this, really I am, but you scared me, you understand that? Really frightened me. What with all that goes on now. You could get into a lot of trouble. You're lucky I don't tell Paul. He'd rip your head off.'

He mumbled something apologetic. She left. Upstairs, his dad explained some things about life and told him to be careful, told him that it was all part of growing up. He slapped Adrian on the shoulder. He said to forget about it. He said, 'She's a bit of alright, though. I'll give you that. I would, too, you know, if anything happened between me and your mother. But it stops here, though, you get me?'

There was a lull for a few weeks. He studiously avoided Susannah. The dog was saved from being walked to death. The editor of the *Melody Maker* received far fewer letters about the downfall of Simple Minds. Summer ended. Adrian went back to school, but at school, somehow, they knew.

They all knew.

They knew it at the first registration class in September. They knew it in assembly and at the Harvest Festival service in the cold church. They knew it in the Sixth Form Centre and on the sports field and the science block and the prefabs out by the boundary. They jeered him in Maths and Further Maths and in Physics and Chemistry and General Studies and on cross-country runs and at football practice. Dave Minto knew. Danny Danskin knew. Nick Galpin knew because he did a town crier impression by the lockers while the second years were coming out of the woodwork room. All the hard kids knew. The swots knew. The middle tier kids knew. The teachers knew. The lab technicians and the secretaries knew. The careers advisor clearly knew and even the private tutor employed to teach Adrian Philosophy knew. Whispers on the top-deck of buses carried the knowledge to the kids in all the other schools who soon knew. The slappers who hung around the school gates in their lace gloves and legwarmers knew. When Adrian participated in an inter-county schools science quiz the geeks on the other teams knew. The headmaster knew and had no doubt informed the Minister for Education and Professor Stephen Hawkins. At his parents' Christmas shindig, Little Viv, Killjoy Killick and Colin and Mandy Teakle knew. The girl with the limp knew. The woman who looked like Brian May in the post office knew. The bloke in the home computing shop in the precinct who wore leather tabards like Avon out of *Blake's 7* knew. When Adrian was interviewed at Oxford, the tutors knew. When he then achieved six As at A-Level he suspected that the examiners knew and had marked him down for it. All the administrators and filing clerks in the insurance office where he'd temped over the summer before he left home knew. The woman at the employment agency with the longs legs and the head and gleaming eye of a heron, she knew. Adrian couldn't get served in pubs like the others because the bar staff always knew. On his first day at the college, when he'd hid at the back of the new intake and listened to Zara Gregory asking her sonorous questions he knew that she already knew, just like everyone else in the room knew that she was to be the Heartbreaker as well as what Adrian had done at the reservoir. The boys along the corridor knew. The unshaven men in donkey jackets and monkey boots flogging the *Socialist Worker* and the Jesus Army loopheads on St. Giles knew. Anthony Christmas knew, and all his lacrosse chums and dining society muckers. Even the lonely kids from Hull and Dundee who no one talked to knew. Elaine Preece had known. Until now the only thing that Adrian had been certain of regarding Elaine Preece was that she had known. Her face knew. Her stance knew. Her entourage knew. They all knew, all of them. They all knew a monstrous, false and ever complicating and drippingly lurid version of what he'd been doing at the reservoir. This is how it had felt, anyway. And as he had spoken to no one and just about believed that his mum and dad had spoken to no one except maybe the psychiatrist – who definitely knew – everyone could know only if one person in particular had lied and lied her head off.

He felt something that he'd never felt about himself. He was stupid. No one, for as long as he could remember had ever suggested that he was stupid. He had been stupid, though. It was stupid, the terror of being known, found out. It had gone, though, last night, suddenly, crushed in on itself like a dead star. None of these people in Café Metz knew. None of them had even acknowledged him or shown any interest in him at all. He felt ordinary, one of the boys, the lad himself as he dithered over whether to buy another beer or preserve the two inches left in the glass. He didn't want to look drunk when Zara arrived. He checked his watch. He'd let his thoughts run for much longer than he realized. She was over an hour and a half late, more than even he could allow her. She might be so much more fashionable than he was but there were limits. She was taking the piss. Maybe he should go and look for her? Following her about could seem creepy and controlling, too possessive too early. He wasn't an idiot or unsophisticated. He wasn't. Not any longer.

The Girl with the Crinkle-Cut Hair said, 'He was asleep when they got him. They had to break down the door.'

'And you say he's from around here?' said the man who'd been reading about black holes.

'A few streets away, yes. It's only a matter of time before they find her, I suppose. It's horrid. It's so awful. And that poor boy, waiting for her to come back.'

The next thing Adrian knew he was half way up Little Pretentious Street with a waitress grabbing at his elbow. He'd rushed out, forgetting the bill and had to stuff a twenty-pound note into her apron, tipping big for the first time in his life. Panting, he came to a halt at the end of the Swan King's street. A crowd was packed in around the house. Police vans and panda cars blocked the road. He was soon in among this crowd, jostling to get to the front, pushing his way past camera crews and press photographers, trying to see Zara, expecting every about-turned blonde to be her, anticipating her in the cigarette-smoking girls, in their tear-streaked faces. Later, he would feel guilty that here he was mentally configuring a scenario whereby Zara had been alerted to the terrible news and overtaken by events had not actually meant to stand him up in Café Metz. She would be here. She would be relieved to see him. Men in white boiler suits carried a series of bankers' boxes stuffed with papers along the garden path. Someone slapped Adrian on the back. It was Gareth.

'Looks like they got him, Addo. They're digging up his garden. If you look out your back window, it's like an archaeological dig. I kept expecting Tutankhamen to come popping up, like.'

From the callbox opposite the mini-market Adrian rang the payphone on Zara's staircase. No one answered. He walked around the block trying to come up with a feasible explanation as to why the police would have arrested the Swan King. The only rational explanation was that the Swan King had after all abducted Elaine Preece. Someone else could have discovered this, or there was an accomplice-turned-informant. It couldn't be, though. It couldn't. Adrian knew that this wasn't true. It was too random. Too far-fetched. The real culprit was still staring them in the face.

He called Zara again. He let the phone ring and ring until a gentleman of the press tapped on the glass booth and moved him on. The take-out burger joint across the road was doing good business for late afternoon.

Back at his house, he stood at the window and watched the white boiler suits come in and out of a large tent they'd erected in the Swan King's garden. The radio news bulletin said that a thirty-six year old man was helping police with their enquiries in the case of missing student Elaine Preece. By the time the six o'clock news appeared on the television, the Swan King had a name: Martin Kipps.

When Adrian knocked on Zara's door that evening she wasn't there, or wasn't answering. A barefoot girl in a Suzie Wong dress and pencils stuck in her hair came out onto the landing and said that she'd not seen Zara all day. He tried to console himself, imagining that distraught after the Swan King's arrest she might well blame him for what was unfolding, seeing as he'd been so certain of the Swan King's innocence. He could explain, though. He could help. This was what he was for now. He searched the college bar and the library, and then made a circuit of the few pubs and bars where he knew she sometimes hung out. During a sweep of Augustus he realized that he didn't know much about her other friendships, apart from the obvious. At the porter's lodge he asked for Anthony Christmas's room number. When Christmas came to his door, the cuffs of a pale pink shirt hung loose at his wrists.

'No, not seen her,' he said.

'Can I come in?' said Adrian. 'I want to apologize, for the other night.'

'Bugger off, matey, I'm in the middle of something.'

He didn't even slam the door in Adrian's face.

Δ

The next morning, Adrian was still at his desk after sitting up all night looking out at the now vacated window opposite. The light over there had been on most of the time and the boiler suits had shuffled in and out, doing what Adrian couldn't tell. When Gareth's hand pressed down on his shoulder Adrian didn't know if he'd been dozing or not. He felt no shock or surprise. He could feel nothing.

Gareth had a bundle of tabloids stuffed under his arm. He sat down on the end of the bed, thumped the pile on his knees and opened *The Daily Express*. Martin Kipps, he declared, was unmarried, teetotal, a recluse, Lecturer in German Philosophy on extended sabbatical after a 'nervous breakdown' and author of what the paper called a 'weird' book entitled *Into the Volcano: Husserl, Heidegger and the Phenomenological Method.*

'If he wrote that,' said Gareth,' he's probably one of those neo-Nazis.'

'Heidegger wasn't a committed Nazi,' said Adrian. 'You can't be expected to anticipate the ramifications of contingent decisions.'

'Leave off. Look, there's a picture here. He used to have violet hair and wear black leather gloves when he gave lectures. Imagine that? His colleagues say he's very quiet but his ex says…she's a nice bit of crackling, look, I'd have her over a fire…she says here he's obsessed with avant-garde poetry…she means porno, right? And he made her see a film called *The Night Porter* three times in one week. It's about shagging in a concentration camp, it says here.'

'He must be guilty then.'

'Neighbours say he stared out of his window all night. Was that you playing Inspector Morse again?'

'No. I know who was, though.'

His legs rigid from sitting still for so long, Adrian had to ease himself out of his chair in little jerks. He walked across the room in the style of a man riding a bicycle with triangular wheels. Gareth found this gut-bustingly funny and was still laughing as Adrian thudded stiffly down the stairs and let himself out of the house. He squinted in the low, sickish light and headed for town.

He found her in the Upper Reading Room. At least he discovered her bag and her books and notepads stacked on a desk not far from where they first met. Drifting along the aisles he scanned the hunched figures scratching away with their pens and thumbing their books. He knew that he must look pale and exhausted, so white that he could easily fade into the margins of any one of the millions of pages there. He turned the corner of the vast L-shaped room. She was at the index files, leant over an extended drawer, flicking through cards and wearing a midnight-blue skating skirt that he'd never seen before. Caught in the light from one of the windows, a golden fuzz of sheen and dust sparkles cascaded from the crest of her hair and across her strong, gazelle-like back and down her bare calves to where it shimmered on the parquet floor. He approached her slowly, trying to smile. Bumping into each other like this. The causal serendipity of boyfriend-girlfriend, of soulmates and confidantes.

Her scarlet nails clicked on the cards, reminding him of how she'd spidered her fingers across his LPs that first night. He leant on the cabinet. His shadow fell over the drawer. She startled.

'Oh Jesus, Adrian.'

'Hello. I've been looking for you everywhere.'

She straightened, took a step backwards and started to look around at the floor for something that clearly wasn't there.

'OK?' he said.

'Fine,' she said.

'Go for a walk?'

She didn't answer and inched further backwards on her heels. As he returned her stare he began to sense that behind her eyes she was no more than cataloguing how shattered and unkempt he looked, and perhaps wondering how talking to him made her appear to the librarians at their desk on the other side of the cabinets.

'It was you, wasn't it?' he said.

'Pardon?'

'You know what I mean.'

'Adrian, I don't.'

'Do you know what being exposed like this will do to someone like him? If anything happens it'll be your fault.' He huffed. 'Look, can we go for a coffee and just talk this through, please?'

She turned sideways to him and slammed the drawer shut. Her hair fell over her face as she leant on the top of the cabinet.

'Please,' he said. 'I missed you yesterday. I did. I was worried. I didn't know what was going on. You didn't show. I need help. I need to help you. Zara? Please come outside with me. Please. This is nothing. This will pass. Please. You know me better than anyone.'

Her shoulder twitched.

She stood up and turning to him seemed ever so tall.

'Adrian, you're a lovely guy.'

'C'mon,' he said. 'Don't be stupid. Let's go outside.'

'Listen, honey, you've just got more invested in this than I have.'

'That's not true.'

'Please don't be excruciating, Adrian.'

Her nose and upper lip creased. In her eyes then, something that he'd never seen in her expression before, something otherwise familiar, that sent pinpricks marching across his scalp.

'Please,' he said.

A librarian at the desk, the man with the black polo neck and Moses-style beard whispered so loudly that his voice sent a frisson through Adrian's knees. She already knew, and now the librarian knew what Adrian was up to and how pathetic he was, knew that he was about to get down on his knees and beg. Adrian started to shift and felt that he was walking backwards, still staring at her and the librarian craning around her at his desk to make sure that the commotion had ceased. Adrian was facing forwards, though, striding up the aisle, towards the great long windows beyond which flagpoles and towers and ramparts spiked up into the sky. Even then he knew she was mistaken. If he stropped off now she would realise this. It would hit her like a ten-ton truck. She would follow.

After he'd turned at the L-bend and headed for the exit he slowed his step and waited for her footfalls to hurry up behind him. He waited for her to call his name, for her to stop him and grab him by the shoulders and tell him, yes, it was true. He did know her better than anyone. There was a rapport between them now, a confidence. She would admit it.

There were no footsteps. The scratchers in the aisles knew this, he could tell, suddenly. The Japanese happy-snappers arranged in front of the statue in the square below knew this as he passed them. The shoppers in Broad Street knew. The men selling the *Socialist Worker* and the Jesus Army loopheads he scurried by on his way home knew. Gareth wasn't in but Gareth no doubt already knew. The people who wrote the stories in the newspapers that Gareth had left in his room knew. By evening they knew something else, too. Elaine Preece's body had been discovered concealed in a chamber beneath the coalbunker in the back garden of the house where Pepper Marx lived.

Sometime in the early evening Adrian turned off the radio. The news programmes had stopped giving out more details after it was announced that Pepper Marx had now confessed to the murder of Elaine Preece. They'd had an argument, apparently. She wanted to end the relationship. He'd lost his temper and throttled her, then panicked and hid the body. The breakthrough in the investigation came when architectural plans of the house where Marx lodged revealed a crawlspace beneath the bunker in the garden. A cadaver dog had barked above it. She was down there, wrapped in a sheet. The family asked for consideration and to be allowed to grieve in private. Pepper Marx was in police custody. Adrian was alone in the house. No movement or chatter came from the other bedrooms. No one was cooking pasta shells in the kitchen. No one sat in the yard and smoked or gossiped. It was dusk, the sky above the houses opposite turning a Prussian blue colour. A breeze ruffled the top of the tent that was still standing in Martin Kipps's garden. The fronds of a laburnum tree in the house next door quivered. He was sitting at his desk, one particular page of one of Gareth's tabloids open in front of him.

It was a picture of Elaine Preece, a close-up of her head and shoulders. She might have been perched on some wall or stile; green fields stretched away behind her. There were hills and conifers. He had seen this picture before. It had been used extensively in the press and on TV since she vanished. It had never seemed quite so real before, this picture of a girl, not yet twenty, lightly-tanned, no hint of apprehension in that smile, in those clear eyes beneath the brim of a salmon-pink sunhat. There was an unguarded contentment in her face as she posed for whoever had taken the photograph, whoever had stood in that field staring into her.

The picture seemed to reform and clarify the longer he looked at it. He did not think, as he had the first time he'd seen this picture that none of this would have happened to her if only she had chosen him to take her photograph on a sunny day in some rustic and romantic setting. He did not feel anger and weakness when he thought about all the lies Pepper Marx had told until now. He did not rage at Zara for believing in Pepper Marx over him. He did not realize, as he would later, that he had been right all along and Zara owed him an apology. He did not yet think that Zara owed Martin Kipps a massive apology. He did not speculate upon the reasons why she had left him on his own, did not yet fret about whether it was because of what he had told her about the reservoir, or whether what she had told him about Mustique had made her feel vulnerable. He did not extrapolate some monstrous version of himself that could not inspire trust and love, as we would do in the subsequent years. He did not yet start to wonder how she was and need to know what she was doing. He did not think about Zara or anything that Zara had said or done or what she had removed and put back on again. He did not think about being right. He did not think about knowledge. He did not feel understood or understanding. He stared at Elaine until each grain and detail seemed to stand out like Braille. He imagined her shaking off her frozen pose and slipping from her perch to feel the damp earth beneath her feet, deciding now whether to look for ammonites buried in the flint wall, or to run with abandon through the woods, find a tarn there and swim.

He realised that they had all been living through an interlude, an anomaly, a disturbance in the arrangement.

When he finally managed to look up from the paper, out across the courtyard, beyond the walls and the tent, up in the window, hanging in a white cube, in the glare of the naked-bulb was the Swan King.

The street was empty. No one sat in parked cars. No crowd confronted Adrian, no journalists or rubberneckers. He pushed his way past no one on his approach to the house. No police constable on the step blocked his ascent. He hesitated on the top step and looked up at the blackening house. In the distance, machinery rumbled.

The Piazza Fontana is a long way off here. In the Piazza Fontana Adrian West will lurk by the statue, a middle-aged man now, watching her and whomever it is she adorns as they trail their ease and satisfaction behind them. It cools, at last, what should have been forgotten here, on this step, in front of my house. In the Piazza Fontana Adrian will count back the years of Pepper Marx's prison sentence. Marx served all of his twenty. He was freed only a few months before Adrian's holiday in Milan and had disappeared back to America. When Marx's release was reported in the papers, for a few weeks afterwards the twenty years kept hissing through Adrian's head. In Piazza Fontana he will use the length of the sentence to work out how long it had been since she spidered her fingertips across the sleeves of his records in his room and took him to breakfast and told him her secret on the night they stared back at me across the courtyard.

When Adrian knocked, I left my post at the window. I went downstairs and opened the door. We sat in the room, many times, over many years, and talked about how to survive. I wanted him to survive. I needed him to. I needed to be effective again.

This is how I know.

This is how I know everything.

Nine Hundred and Ninety Something

– Nick Sweeney –

The sea was lapping with some contentment round the harbour at Bakirköy, known as the Marina. A bit of a paradox, as the Marina welcomed no seafaring vessels, only drinkers to populate its bars that kidded you into thinking they were places in, I don't know, Cape Cod, or Key Largo. At seven on a Sunday morning, they looked forlorn, as did my friend Don Darius. He gripped my arm and fixed alarmed eyes on me, and said, 'Where am I?'

Turquoise May morning down by the Marmara Sea, I could have said, but I was in no mood for poetry. 'Outdoor bar on hard seats,' it was my misfortune to remind him.

'It's Damn Bull.'

'You're damn right.'

Being the kind of guy who can be happy in a place like Istanbul, I only appeared to be agreeing with him. Don, I knew, had issues with the place. 'My wish to be here is cancelled forthwith,' he was telling people, like, a day after arriving.

I hadn't met any interesting girls at the Saturday night party we had been to – or that is, I had, but didn't get into pole position for popping the old feather bed question – so had wound up in that unenviable have-to-stay-over-with-an-asshole situation. In this case, an asshole who had not only lost the key to his gaff, but with a room-mate who was away for the weekend.

I changed the subject, a little, said, 'It's damn cold, anyhow,' though in fact, it wasn't, not really, and there was a kindly sun on our faces.

Despite the hour, there were guys around, walking. Most times in Istanbul, and in all Turkish cities, guys walk. I don't know where they walk, which isn't important – *they* don't know where they walk. What they don't do is stay in the crowded houses they have, on account of living with their parents till they marry, then immediately having a wife and, like, five kids, plus those same parents and in-laws. Those guys like to walk, but even more than that they like to stop, see what other guys are doing. Our Sunday-morning rousing under a canopy out front of a bar would almost certainly draw a crowd of rubberneckers who would ask us, and with good reason, what in the name of God we were doing there.

'I think we ought to go eat.' My suggestion was a typical Midwest solution to a lack of any other courses to pursue.

Don said something like, 'Ugh-hugh-hugh-gugh.'

'Exactly. So where?'

I lived in Tarabya, which was maybe twenty kilometres up the Bosphorus, so I didn't know Bakirköy. Don was convinced there was a café on the main drag that would be open, though that turned out not to be true. However, as we stood outside looking foolish, we heard a rattle of shutters opening nearby, and immediately smelt coffee, and made a Pavlovian lope around a corner.

'That was not my first experience of napping outdoors,' Don announced as we horsed down our chow. 'It was not even my only experience this *year* of sweet outdoor dreams and not even a crib for a bed.'

'Oh?' My interest was partly reluctant. 'So tell.'

He began grandly, 'I was in Katowice in the winter vacation. You know where that is?'

'Yeah,' I claimed, and he hovered over that, letting me have full pause to say, 'Well, that is, not exactly.' But I knew it had to be someplace in the east of Europe, a scratchy name like that.[1]

'It's in Poland,' he enlightened me. 'South of Poland, the like throbbing hub of its industrial centre, to be precise.' I stopped Don from

---

[1] Kat-oh-vit-zeh.

giving me a map reference. He said, 'I was there to interview for a job. I am a Pole,' he declared.

'Oh,' I said, 'okay,' but thought, yeah, and I am a cross-eyed virgin from a Swiss finishing school.

'Your name's Finney,' he digressed. 'Correct me if I'm wrong, but that's Irish, right?'

'Right.' The word fooled him into a smug nod. 'I'll correct you,' I went on. 'It's French. Huguenot, in fact.'

I realize that the being ethnic schtick is a thing that appeals to some Americans. To me, it just shows an unhealthy preoccupation with a past that spattered into the water all misspelled at places like Ellis Island. I don't care which part of Europe was inhospitable to my ancestors. What matters to me is right now, and tomorrow. And, often, breakfast.

'When I say I'm a Pole,' Don said, 'I mean from my family.'

'Uh-huh.'

'Grandparents, and all.'

'No kidding.'

'Where was I?'

'That was your excuse.'

'What?'

'For being in a place like Katowice.'

'Ah-hah, right, yes. Well, like I said, I interviewed there. I am going to give up this current...*ordeal* in this damn town and teach in Poland next school year.'

'Oh, yeah.' That came back to me from a conversation out of which we'd been distracted the previous night, once we had gotten taken along with the whole party thing. 'Poland.'

'*Anyhow.*' The stress on the word betrayed Don's anxiety, that of the true raconteur, at being adrift from his tale. 'What happened was I got to Katowice in the late evening. When I got there, the guy I was supposed to meet, guy from the school, wasn't at the bus station. He had been there, of course, but was told by the bus company that the bus I was on would be two hours behind schedule. He quite reasonably went home, intending to come back later.'

What I kept doing was taking part in the conversation from here on in, and yet not doing so, by making the usual conversational grunts and nods and *uh-huhs* and *rights*, so I am not going to document them anymore. You will just have to imagine them.

'My bus wasn't two hours late,' Don told me. 'It was forty five minutes late, only. Everybody had been misinformed. I watched people at the bus station, and even asked a few likely-looking guys whether they were waiting for a frozen Texan. They weren't. What I did was put my bag in the station lock-up. What I did then was wander in town till I found a bar. This was in an old hotel, which, far as I could see, no longer had guests. The bar had tall tall windows hung with long long drapes which were dark, but no colour I can recall now. It had chandeliers which, for all their folderol, did not give out much light at all.'

His description was good, but Don forgot to tell me about the gold that moved in the heart of the place, and illuminated it.

'A waitress came and took my order,' Don resumed. 'She wore a white shirt and a black skirt that made her walk in a stiff-legged way. She wore white pantyhose which, in my opinion, didn't go too well with her very hairy legs.'

I saw her. She was an old-style waitress from communist times. She didn't give a goddam whether people ate there or not, or enjoyed their food or not.

'The beer was good in that place,' Don remembered. 'It was good.' I watched him thinking ferociously about that beer as he looked at the little glass of tea in his hand. 'It was good beer. I asked for another, and it was brought, and I saw that it was good too.' There was no mileage in that for him, so he took a sip of his tea and continued, and, because there was a lot of this kind of stuff in his good narrative, I am going to continue telling the story for him from here.

In that tall hotel bar room in Katowice, Don sat and drank and ate. So engrossed was he in his beer and vittles that he didn't notice tables filling. He had the weight of his thoughts to get on with. It was no passing impression he wanted to give in Katowice; he didn't just want a job there: he wanted a change of life, wanted out of Istanbul, and in to the Poland from which his family hailed before they became common old Texans. It's taken for granted among people I know now that language schools in places like Poland, and especially in towns like Katowice, that are not easy on the eye under a century of industrial glop, are crying out for native speakers of English, even Texans. They would have taken Don had he given them a call the night before start of term and said, 'Hey, I think I'll just mosey on over and work at your school, okay?' But he wasn't to know that, then. Also, like the Southern gentleman he is, he wanted to do things properly, didn't want anybody grizzling, 'Did you ever hear the like of that Don Darius, just breezing up out of nowhere and demanding a job with his fancy Texas ways?' Finally, he was burning to see the land of his ancestors for the first time.

The people who came in and filled those tables while Don chewed and supped were what used to be called Gypsies. In most of Europe, people call them *cigane*, pronounced (and sometimes spelled) *tzigany*. This is a Byzantine name, apparently. The respectful name to call them, and the name they call themselves, is *Roma*. I don't want to offend anybody who reads this, so I am going to use the hybrid word *Romanies*, that being one name I was brought up to call them. If I ever talk to one I will ask him or her what she or he would like to be called in the unlikely event of ending up in another of my stories.[2] There were four Romany men, and maybe eight women, scattered round three tables.

They weren't the Romanies you might imagine, with a bright waggon outside. I mean, they wore regular clothes, no gaudy scarves or vests, or anything. The guys were in a huddle. The women laughed with a quiet grace. Don noted them, and went back to his thoughts.

After a minute, he was interrupted respectfully by one of the guys, who asked in broken English if he could sit down a second. Don bade him sit, and was surprised to see that two of them did so. They faced him across his table, and pointed at his beer and his food, enquired, 'Good?'

With no more preamble, a bag was brought up onto the table, and a package was pulled out and opened to reveal an antique flintlock pistol. Did Don want to buy it?

'I don't hold with firearms,' Don assured me. He also had no connection with the oil business, didn't possess a pair of hand-tooled cowboy boots and had never ridden a horse; it was a thing of his, to avoid walking the world as a Texas cliché.

He didn't pick the pistol up when invited. He kept his no-thank-you polite, even though having to repeat it maybe ten times. He didn't doubt the gun's provenance; he had no problem believing that it had been in their family since a several-times-removed great-great uncle had been press-ganged into the army of that short-assed megalomaniac Napoleon. But he didn't want it. The price plummeted, but Don still didn't want it. They thanked him for his time and withdrew to their table, and broke out into quiet conversation. The women called, asked the men things, looked

---

[2] I've met native Americans who wanted to be called *injuns*; I worked with a guy in a wheelchair who called himself a crip; right there in Istanbul I knew a gay guy who referred to himself and his pals as *fags*; I ran into a Nebraskan one time who called himself a Kraut. I sometimes get a little confused with this.

over slyly at Don. There is stuff that goes down among the Romanies that delineates men's business and women's business, and Don thought the sharp words that ensued may have been to do with this. They disputed merrily for a time, and then were quiet.

Don is an incurable sender of postcards. I don't think he actually believes he's in some burg unless he can tell the folks back wherever about it. It was his habit to buy and write them as soon as he hit a place, knowing well that the rest of his time could be such a frenzy of sightseeing and beer swallowing that he might have neither time nor coherence nor inclination.[3] He got out a stack of them at that table, and scribed away. Then he ordered another beer. The waitress slammed it down on his table, and told him something in grave tones. He didn't understand. A guy appeared behind the *babooshka* to explain that she was telling him that this would have to be his last beer, and could he settle up, as she wanted to go home and…shave her legs, or something. Don thanked the guy, took a bulging billfold out, and paid.

Maybe he shouldn't have taken the billfold out in front of people, though, as ever, it was his putting it back that told the real tale.

The Samaritan translator also clutched a beer. This guy was a chunky fifty or so, in leather jacket, bluejeans and scuffed shoes. He told Don he might as well join him, and Don didn't protest. The man's English was good. After asking Don the usual where-are-you-from and what-brings-you-to-this-hellhole questions, he reciprocated with his own unremarkable story, which was that he was a truck driver from Essen, in Germany. He delivered stuff to Katowice once a month. It was a dump. There was not much to do in town. Only one decent place around, he attested, and it was right under that end-of-empire room in which they sat.

Down there was a club with the best beer in all Poland. It stayed open late. A guy could get very lucky there with the ladies. Did Don follow?

Don answered the sixty four thousand dollar question wrong, and soon found himself trooping out of the building and into its nether regions via a side door over whose lintel spluttered the neon words *Star Klub*. Don took out that billfold again and paid the guy on the door, and because his German pal had been such a mensch, he paid for him, too.

---

[3] Don's cards always look like the crappy ones you get at bus or train stations. This is because they actually *are* the crappy ones you get at bus or train stations.

The first thing Don noticed as his eyes got used to the dim light was that the Star Klub was maybe the size of two bathrooms. There were two tables, maybe three. The bar didn't feature any beer at all, let alone the best in all Poland. That was Don's first disappointment. To salve it he ordered one of the local vodkas. The trucker paid. That was nice. They talked, elbows on the bar, asses on high stools. When Don turned his head, the place was full of Romany women.

They were pretty, some of them. Some of them made eyes at Don. They started to shimmy to the music. The German guy winked, and nudged Don.

Now Don didn't head for a dancefloor in Katowice to hook up with a Romany woman, no matter how pretty. He would be the first to say he didn't know much about Romanies, but even he knew that only children mortally offended by parents ever dreamed of running away with them, and that nobody went home with their women, no sir. When they sirened him into the dance, it was a little bit of fun – it hit the romantic in him; you know: *went to Poland, danced with the raggle-taggle Gypsies-oh.* That might have been the tale he had fixed on telling.

He took his jacket off, left it on a chair, and became a dancing fool.

'I was hot,' he explained. He always said that when he told this tale. People said, 'You were...*hot?*'[4] He was dancing; he got hot, he took his jacket off. He got hotter, drank more cold vodkas, the Essen trucker setting them up on the bar for him each time he wanted a breather. This went on for some time whose boundaries later eluded Don.

The first inkling he had that something was wrong was when he wobbled out of an expert John Travolta pirouette and saw white rectangles on the floor near the tables. It wasn't a vodka assault on his eyes; nor had anybody cut holes in the dark carpet to reveal whitewash. They were the postcards he had left in his jacket pocket. The jacket also lay on the floor. To nobody in particular, he said, 'Hey.'

When he *did* want to get particular, there was nobody there with whom to get particular or otherwise. His dancing queens were gone. He looked round for his German pal, and saw that he was just an empty shot glass on the bar.

---

[4] Don didn't mean turned on sexually – he's from smalltown Texas. When they say *hot* down there, they just mean opposite of *cold.* Or maybe use it about a good pedal steel guitar player. But that's about it, I think.

He reached down and picked up his jacket. When he'd last checked, it had held a billfold with some Polish money, a little Turkish money, several credit cards, and nine hundred and ninety something dollars. When he mentioned that, people looked at him as if he had just announced that he had changed his name to Kennedy and was going to run for president. The billfold was gone. Don stomped up the stairs to the street, and saw a Skoda van about to be gone too. He lunged at it and kicked its door, but the discussion was doomed to be dismissed in the coughing and farting of an old but trustworthy engine.

The rest didn't serve much purpose. He went back down to the bar and remonstrated with the woman behind it, who claimed to understand nothing. Did he want anything more to drink? If not, her look suggested, she'd get to bed with a book. The deejay sauntered over, but the only English he knew was from pop tunes, or so he claimed.[5] The guy from the door showed his face. He knew no English, either. None of them wanted the police there, but Don insisted, so they called, and they waited, silent and brooding, with them all pissed at Don and Don in turn pissed at them.

The police arrived. They yelled a little at the gathered staff of the Star Klub, a bit like those scenes in Agatha Christie books when the detective exposes the perpetrator, but no butler stepped forward to confess. Official fingers were waggled, drawing only faces of hurt innocence.

'But it's all a scam,' Don roared at the Keystone Copskis. 'They're all in on it.'

'We know,' one of the cops replied calmly.

'Then – but – ah – so – can't you –'

Nope, they couldn't. Had to catch them at it, like in anyplace in the world.

Don continued to alternate between speechless and incoherent, but none of it made a difference of even a little goddam. He had to go make a statement at the police station, just so he could back up an insurance claim, but that would happen next day. As he left the club, he spotted his postcards once again, and picked them up, pocketed them. Maybe they

---

[5] Some wicked people in Istanbul made up conversations Don might have had with the deejay, along the lines of "They stole my money." "*Yesterday all my troubles seemed so far away.*" "You got to do something." "*We got to install microwave ovens.*" "I need to call the police." "*It's another day for you and me in Paradise.*" Etcetera, etcetera, etcetera. Not good. And not funny. Most of the time.

helped keep him warm as he spent the night in a doorway someplace near the station.[6]

Don didn't let his loss faze him for too long. He snored the night away in the absolute certainty that nobody was going to take his dough. The cold soon dropped from his bones when he turned up at the school at the crack of eight; they let him take a shower and get hot soup and bread down him, let him interview and declared him fit and insane enough to work there the following year. People there helped him get money wired from the States, credit cards cancelled, new ones issued. Then he forgot it. That's the kind of guy Don is. It didn't matter that he was down near-enough a grand; he was wide-eyed and smiling among his own people, and that was what he fixed on for the rest of his visit.

In that café in Bakirköy, Don finished his jeremiad, which brought a chill to my bones, so well did he tell it. It soon lifted with the ingestion of good food and hot tea. We'd only crashed outdoors for maybe three hours, and May in Istanbul was when it was just getting seriously warm. I said how in any case wouldn't he agree that Istanbul wasn't all bad? If only from the point-of-view of outdoor sleepers? He had to go for that, and a feeling of magnanimity got him to admit that our breakfast was making the world a fine place, for a time, at least.

I had my own buddies up my end of the Bosphorus, and Don wasn't a close friend. I saw him a few times more that school year, in bars in town, but he was so comprehensively drunk he barely recognized me. All the same, last time we met he gave me his future address and urged me to wander over the wastes to see him in Poland if I got the inclination.

'Fat chance,' I told myself, but I shook his hand and said not to rule it out.

A wanderlust grabbed me on the cusp of winter vacation the following year. I whizzed Don a card, got him to call me, and it was arranged and, after a day on trains, there I was, in a winter town from an old movie; black with coal dust or white with snow, and no colours in between.

---

[6] Mine was one of the ones he wrote out in the tall room, and it says: Fine beer, good food, home n dry n having a time so far. I think I might get very lucky here, boy. Well, ouch.

Don was perfect to stay with; his teaching job kept him busy, and out of my hair a lot of the time. He also had a sweet girlfriend, and she kept him occupied too. He and I did two days in Warsaw, but I went solo on daytrips to Krakow, went to see other places, like holy Czestochowa, and horrendous Auschwitz.

On my last evening in Katowice I arranged to meet with Don at a place in the town centre. We'd make a night of it, we'd promised. I was back at the station late from that day's trip, and I didn't want the hassle of riding the tram to Don's just for an hour, so I went in search of a bite. I walked into a place. The waitress padded up the room and threw a menu at me. I knew the score on eating out in Poland by then, and instead of painstakingly reading through the lists and choosing something they didn't have, I asked what they did have, and ordered it.

It was then I noticed how hairy the waitress's legs were under her white pantyhose. I looked up at the tall drapes, squinted at the dusty chandeliers with their one-out-of-five bulbs working. I looked around, and saw that four, maybe five Romany women were sitting at two tables, watching me frankly. They made tinkly laughs to themselves. *Antique pistol*, I remembered. Where was it?

My grub came. I ate. After maybe ten minutes a guy came strolling down the room, carrying a glass of beer. Leather jacket, hair in a part, fifty, maybe. He did such a good job of ignoring the Romany women that I almost applauded. Before he could open his mouth I wished him, '*Guten Abend.*'

He echoed it, in some surprise. This didn't stop him enquiring, 'American?' though, once he'd pulled a chair out, scraped it back and sat down.

I nodded. I did a lot of that. Most of my high school German was lying forgotten someplace. Anyhow, I wanted to hinder him with a language barrier. I let him go through his paces: trucker, check, German, check, from Essen, delivering stuff to Katowice one time a month – blah blah: it all checked. But what could I do with it? I was meeting Don at a place a ten-minute walk away, and I didn't know another soul in town that I could call.

'Any cool places around here,' I asked my new pal, 'where I could, you know, go dancing, sink a brewski, meet a nice *Fräulein?*'

He knew just the place.

'It's downstairs,' I cued him, 'right?'

He nodded slowly, and I could see he was wondering whether to do pleased or puzzled.

'That was my pal,' I was about to say, plus a whole lot of other things that blared a Babel in my head.

But I realized: it wasn't personal. They weren't on a mission to destroy Don Darius's faith in human nature, nor to stop him from going into bars alone and striking up conversations with strangers. Don did the same bar-stooling and the same spieling, and his fool's dancing was eternal. He called the Romanies by their preferred name, and not *thieving Gypsies*. He stopped often in the street in Katowice and handed grubby banknotes to begging Romany women. It wasn't personal, that night in the cold a year before: they just wanted the gold.

I had to junk the personal response.

Then it hit me, though, that I was potential patsy number whatever in a series longer than *Dallas*. That could have made it personal, alright. Could I call the cops and tell them a scam was in process? With my five words of Polish, it was unlikely. Even if I could, would that drag them out of the donut shop?

'You will come?' Herr Trucker was asking me.

'They sell the best beer in all Poland there?' I enquired.

'Yes. Very good beer.'

'The Star Klub, right?' I didn't wait for his answer. 'I had a pal went there one time,' I told him in slow German. 'Yeah. He spent...now let me get this right...nine hundred and ninety dollars.'

The guy forced out a pack-of-Marlboro-a-day laugh.

'Good time, right? Blow nine hundred and ninety dollars in one evening? Huh? What do you say to that, pal?'

He could hear and understand me fine, and what was more he was sharp enough to have gotten exactly what I was saying; it was a magic number that any hustler would remember out of all the nickels-and-dimes jobs. That was why his mind was half-fixed on moving on. He had his legs half-swivelled round to make his way out, had his billfold in his hand and was pulling a few banknotes out. I reached out and grabbed his wrist. He looked pointedly at my hand, then at the rest of me, sizing me up. He looked pretty confident that I wasn't the kind of guy who'd be prepared to cut up rough with truckers. He was right. And yet there was a kind of panic in his face, and I addressed that look and whatever lay behind it, saying, 'Listen. I *know* what happened.' He pulled his wrist away sharply, knocking his beer over onto the crotch of his pants, and that got him to his feet, telling me I was crazy.

'Hey,' I vamped, 'sorry.' I grabbed handfuls of napkins and pressed them into his hands, and, not knowing entirely what to make of this turn of events, he put a lot of effort into assuring me that he was fine, and that, in fact, he had to get going.

It might have been just fancy on my part, but I thought a look passed then between the trucker and the Romany women. Not too hurriedly, they pulled coats on and made a procession down the room.

'Hey, listen.' I pushed my luck in a further attempt at getting back to our conversation, but the guy really did have to hit the road, the pace he was making. He slapped banknotes down on the waitress's table, and then I was alone. I sat and watched the last of the spilled beer trickle toward me, then got up before it hit me.

Those beautiful Romany women danced for emperors, for caravan kings on the Silk Routes, danced for bandits who robbed those same caravans and made those kings less than nothing. They danced for gold before men who'd slogged and raged and travelled and built and destroyed and killed and conquered and arranged their daughters' marriages to get more gold. When it came to fools, they didn't dance for them; they danced *with* them, and just took the gold. Those women didn't stash it in banks, but wore it on their necks and wrists and hands, in their ears and noses, to let the world know that maybe it hated them, but all the same they had its gold.

That was the gold I saw in the old hotel bar in Katowice. When the women left, it was gone.

The waitress was glaring at me. She flicked the lights on and off once, then padded past me to the windows and started opening the drapes. All the other colours leached out of the room, except for the tan square of the trucker's billfold on the floor near a leg of my table.

The street moved with homegoing people, their heads down, their feet quick. In the hotel's doorway, I pulled out the family photos and gasoline receipts, the ID card and driver's license, stepped back into the lobby and strewed them across the table there, followed them with the billfold itself. I kept only the large bundle of German and Polish banknotes. I didn't bother counting them, just went off to find Don Darius to get him to help me do that black-and-white town a favour, and paint some red all over it.

The Poets of Radial City

– Paul A. Green –

A Cultural Epicentre

Visitors to Radial City can enjoy a wealth of cultural activity. Whether you're tempted by orchestral tournaments at the Polyphonic Hall, a *vernissage* at the Medusa Galleries or a guided walk around the City's Time-Tableaux, you'll discover a constantly changing world of artistic creativity. The City's famous sidewalk cafes – the Cafe Bourgeois, the Helicon – are alive day and night with aesthetic and intellectual debate.

If you prefer more sensuous delights, you can taste the pleasures of cabaret, dance and performance art in the Hospitality District at exclusive clubs like the Dancing Ghost or vibrant gritty venues like Uncle Bonnie's.

And wherever you go, you'll hear music, from concerts at the Beaverdale Stadium by electrical guitar bands like the famous Memes, discovered here by Astral-FM, to the plangent pipes of picaresque Ruralist minstrels wandering the precincts of the Basilica of St Barnabas.

But the literary *flaneur* will have an especially rich trove to explore, given the City's diverse literary heritage and its ongoing pulse of poetic invention. If you're a lover of traditional verse you're certain to make a pilgrimage to the Rupert Housby-Smith Museum in the Bungalow District, where the poet's manuscripts and model tram collection are lovingly displayed. If you want to enjoy the challenge of current literary trends, browse through the poetry bins at the Underground Bookshop or the Word Hoard. Better still, attend the readings and launches at clubs like Quibbles or the Poetry Lounge, where you can mingle with the *auteurs* and discover the latest literary sensation.

All the cultural industries of Radial City are, of course, indebted to the enlightened sponsorship of both the private sector – Beaverdale Securities, Astral Corp, the Organ Exchange – and the public sector, where the Bureau has kept up-to-date with the most recent artistic developments, notably in literary journals. (From: *The Beginner's Guide to Radial City* – second edition)

Notes on Contributors

Hermia Van de Graeff: Chair of the Radial Artists' Circle. She is preparing a monograph on the orb-painter Arnold Toobey. This edition of RADIANCE© marks her debut as a poet.

Charles Kenning: Recognised as the last living link with the Bungalow Poets, Kenning recently edited *An Arbour for Augustus – Selected Poems of Rupert Housby-Smith*. His own collection *Odes and Gnomics* will shortly be appearing with the Claudian Press.

Hilbert Carraway: His new book *Silicate Zombies* from Fast Breeder Books has just won the Norbert Prize.

Nirvana Lux: Formerly lead vocalist with the Close-Fitting Girls, her books include *Mashing the Monster* and *The Uranium Cookbook*.

Hereward Neubauer: 'Poetry is blood, incense and toil,' states Neubauer. In addition to verse, he has published the fantasy saga *Dungor Lord of the Tidal Flats* and is writing a biography of the late Randolph Lubbock.

Igna Beth Bosanquet: Her new collection *The Volcanoes of Parnassus* will be launched at a civic reception at the Polyphonic Hall. She teaches Creative Writing at Radial University.

Rochlitz Fusilio: Recently published in Seizures, Monkey Puzzle, Dancing Jumbo, Frooti's Private Journal, Trashbot, The Traction Worker, and Quirks for Quarks.

Maisie Obadiah: A social worker on attachment to the Hospitality District, Maisie is founder of the Radial Victims Support Group. Her poems have appeared in *Stewpot*, *Tompion Times*, and *Fiery Serpent*.

P.V.Glotz: His CD *Roaring Fit to Burst* is forthcoming on Top Secret Records after his recent controversial appearance at Tongues Untied, together with a new book *Dynaflow Shag* available from Glotz Publications or via the Lobe at the usual address.

Ibrahim F. Spruill: His chap-book *The Cow with the Long Shadow* has just been published by Broken Spear Booklets. He is Poet-in-Residence at the Psychiatric Institute.

Tybalt Turner: His first collection *Ripping the Frazzle!* arrives soon from Cryptographix Inc.

Jack Hague: Formerly Poetry Instructor at the Urban College, now occasional presenter for Astral-FM. His poems have appeared in *Overmole* and *Screaming Fish*.

Millie Honeycutt: Millie's poems have been published in *Versicles*, *Running Fox*, *Amythyst*, and *The Oakdene Review*. She enjoys entertaining and dance.

The Editorial Board of RADIANCE © wish to thank all their friends and sponsors for financial assistance in producing and distributing this issue.

Bureaucrats of the Indeterminate Interval

'Dr. Morphy isn't happy...' Esmond Van de Graeff doesn't want to hear this, but his new Supervisor, the stocky red-faced Serena Quarmby, won't let him leave the room until he takes the folder she's thrusting into his hand. 'I thought your team had matters at Radiance under control.'

'Infiltrating these poetry circles is a very delicate matter. Particularly when one's wife is an unwitting operative.' He still feels queasy about involving Hermia in the operation. But when she'd announced an ambition to write sonnets, he realised that this was a unique opportunity for the Bureau to probe the City's literary world, source of so many subversive whorls and fluxes in the urban probability flow. 'We have to be patient. Hermia will eventually reinforce the stabilising influences when she joins the editorial board. But it's taken her eleven submissions just to get her first acceptance. Anyway, old Kenning is a safe pair of hands. He's publishing sound people like Neubauer and Miss Bosanquet.'

Serena Quarmby pulls a copy of the magazine from the folder and fans it under his nose. 'Nonsense! Kenning's losing it. His eclecticism has gone mad. Does he ever read the contributions? Look at this…'

Van de Graeff scans the elaborate radial patterns reticulating the glossy pinkish cover. For a micro-second he envisions exposed brain tissue, a flash-forward that nearly sickens him, but she's flipping the thick pages.

'See? Carraway…that repellent Glotz…Fusilio…and the little hooligan Tybalt Turner! Think of how work like that could tweak the City's indeterminacy factor…It was your job to check all this out. Morphy wants a full report by Monday! You can start with that dubious Carraway.'

Hilbert Carraway – Vectoring the Zombies 1

flounced by rotted grain
nebules of the skyways
vector all zombies now

they was disgorging a pinky slot
playing out the airmiles
out of fossils, grubs, and lovelies

so get your selves carried right away
on a raft of sheds
a bloat will frill your sensimilla

Officer Van de Graeff wishes he'd never asked for a temporary internal transfer to the Textual Analysis Unit. He thought that browsing the printed page would make a pleasant change from sitting in front of Portal screens all night, squinting for the tell-tale streaking of Probability Wave traces as drunks staggered out of the clubs down Baphomet Street – unaware, of course, of how their lurching gait could so have easily toppled into the abyss of the Polyverse…He is confident in simple tasks, like monitoring the front page of *The Radial Times* to ensure that the reportage of those increasingly frequent 'electrical accidents' isn't marred by wild speculation. He had no difficulty, either, in checking that Hereward Neubauer's latest *Dungor* saga kept to a robust linear narrative, with all the polysemy effectively neutralised. He's been well trained in data-mining sub-texts. Nevertheless, these latest utterings from the Poets of Radial City challenge all his crypto-poetic skills.

He fingers the creamy paper, then traces the lines with his index finger, as if he could stroke the meaning out of them. So the 'nebules' were 'flounced by rotted grain…'

'Nebules' could be capsules of salbutamol fluid, vaporised in a nebuliser for treating respiratory complaints like asthma. But these are 'nebules of the skyways' – perhaps a peculiar metaphor for 'nebulae' – star-clouds? Or sky-capsules – a reference to the City's ancient mythologies of alien flight-craft? Which could be vaporised by the radiance of the City…

He returns to the first line. 'Flounce' suggests an expression of disdain, perhaps effeminacy – maybe an echo of to 'trounce' or defeat. Defeat by 'rotted grain', which could be a synecdoche for alcohol, notably the cheap lethal brews best avoided in the Hospitality District. But there is a darker allusion, surely, to the Agrarian Belt Ways around the City, farmed by the despised Rurals, who generate most of the urban food supply. Is there a threat of wheat-fungus? Or will the Rurals let their produce rot, rather than pay the depressed prices offered on the urban market-place? He senses some definite pre-cog tremors here.

Then there's the problem of the 'zombies' in the first verse. They are, of course, the living dead, a fairly obvious signification for his fellow-citizens. But there's an overt imperative to 'vector' them, putting them on a convergent collision course and forcing them ultimately in one direction – clearly into some kind of extreme situation.

The sense of impending rupture is only reinforced by the singular/plural mismatch between pronoun and verb in the following line, typical of the restricted verbal codes of the Rurals. Yet the subject 'they' isn't explicitly anchored. Maybe it refers instead to the 'zombies'. And '…disgorging a pinky slot…' is worrying. A 'pinky slot' might refer to a 'pinky' or finger in a 'slot' or slot-machine that disgorges cash – but here the slot itself is somehow disgorged, playing out – or paying out – tokens of virtual affluence in the form of air-miles – flying in 'the nebules of the sky-ways'?

Or the 'pinky slot' could, he supposes, be a crude coinage for the vagina. But how could one be 'disgorged'? He consults the thesaurus for variants – and realises that the term could also mean yield or give up ('funds, esp. funds that have been dishonestly acquired'). So the zombies, those cake-walking dead, were yielding – in the past imperfect – a (collective) and fraudulently acquired vagina?

Now there's a faint distraction, some pulse of ancient lust stirring – playback of a hot night decades ago in the Hospitality District, a woman with sooty eye-shadow, huge pale breasts, his leering Officer Cadet companions nudging him to hand over the sweaty money and go up her crooked stairs. He'd faltered, the impulse passed, they all blundered on to the next bar, and twenty months later he'd married Hermia. But what if – a tiny screen flickers in his brain, like an overlay on his spectacles: *he's now scrawny and bearded, bad skin, pecking at a typewriter in a damp-stained garret, floor covered in brown bottles and bills, his latest buxom service-maid lounging on a mattress…*

Officer Van de Graeff shakes his head, shakes out the false-memory syndrome. He shakes out 'fossils, grubs, and lovelies'. He blanks a neural network, turns on the desk lamp and squints into the blur of signifiers. He's already working hard, working himself out, himselves…

A Wealth of Activity

Hermia Van de Graeff wishes that Esmond didn't have to stay on late at the Bureau. He's been so keen recently to attend literary soirees and her new friend Igna Beth's book-launch is one of the grandest the City has ever known. Already the stalls of the Polyphonic Hall are beginning to fill up. Igna Beth has just arrived on the arm of Charles Kenning, still dapper at seventy-five in his cream linen suit. He escorts the poetess to the podium and fusses over a water-carafe while she casts off her cloak and thumbs through a pristine copy of *Volcanoes of Parnassus*. Igna's long jaw and shoulder-length red hair, combined with her fashionable wimple and leather boots, inspire awe in Hermia, who feels she should be assisting in the forthcoming rite, maybe re-arranging the carnations around the lectern, but she's sitting on a side aisle and doesn't want to draw attention to herself, as a relative newcomer to this exciting milieu.

In the row behind, a *basso profundo* exclamation: 'This hall – a model of Neo-Triumphalist architecture! How Rupert would have loved its restoration!' Hereward Neubauer, mighty in beard, is lecturing a slight blonde woman in pink, Millie Honeycutt, who looks younger than her photo. Hereward points out features of interest – that gothic barrel-vaulting, Corinthian pillars, those Egyptian style architraves, the panelling in ochre and green, while Millie's gaze moves mutely round the complex volumes that enclose this murmuring congregation. Hereward grips her sleeve and draws her closer.

'Compare this with the blank black towers and pyramids of the Fatlands. Little wonder heroics are declining across the City. The young oscillate between anomie and priapism, for aspiration is not encoded for them in a geometry of living stone.'

'It's very sad,' agrees Millie, warily. She leans forward and turns to Hermia. 'Do you know when it's starting?'

It may well have started, for Charles Kenning is now standing several feet away from the microphone, enthusing inaudibly to the murmuring audience. A tech serf ambles on and adjusts the mic stand.

' – granting us the honour of sharing the lyric moment with us all. In a time of alleged indeterminism, as a million delusive gateways open to ensnare the poetic artificer, Igna Beth Bosanquet offers us closure. At a juncture when some persons insist that *poesis* is a mere verbal assemblage, she distils its human essence as a true ambrosial for the spirit. Ladies and gentlemen, I give you – '

The applause ripples as Hermia fumbles in her handbag for a pad and pencil. She's just remembered that Esmond asked her to make notes.

Hilbert Carraway – Vectoring the Zombies 2

so get your selves carried right away
on a raft of sheds
a bloat will frill your sensimilla

basting the queen's tummy in hot lead!
a dream worn like a new eye socket
was committed by the committee

the whoopee baskets of raw tissue
fatted the feast but will fast-forward
last of the great wifettes

laser entanglements
scramble martyrs at six o clock
vector all zombies now

Officer Van de Graeff is weary. The darkened office shimmers around him as he holds the magazine close to the desk lamp, as if tilting it at a new angle would spill out the hidden significations of the text.

He ponders 'a bloat', the surfeit perhaps of an overdose at the neighbourhood meat-bars – but how would this embellish, in a somewhat gendered or feminised way, the ingestion of rare imported cannabis? Or maybe 'frill' is a proletarian street version of 'thrill' – generating more connotations of excess hedonism. His throat is hoarse and his eyes itch.

The next stanza hits him with a great wave of nausea. The intimate colloquialism of 'tummy', the culinary connotations of 'basting', the implications of 'hot lead' either as liquid metal or bullets – the aggregate effect is sickeningly violent. But why the curious noun 'queen'? The Bureau has been administering Radial City as long as he or anyone can remember, despite a few picturesque alt.histories that have been quickly taken out of circulation, via the Great Fire at the Underground Bookshop, one of his first assignments as a young man. Nevertheless, a regal basting was undertaken by 'the committee'. The Bureau has many committees...What is Hilbert Carraway probing here? And Carraway obviously = 'carried away...' Van de Graeff's getting carried away, away. He stops, drops the journal and leans across his desk to retch violently into a wastebasket. His head is throbbing. The play on the 'worn' eye socket has made him squeamish.

Nevertheless he won't give up. He owes it to Hermia to work this through, to work towards his pension, funding a last extension on the bungalow as retirement beckons. More imagery of glut and overload, hints of juvenile, even puerile japes – surely a 'whoopee basket' is related to the equivalent cushion – and this basket hastens some kind of matrimonial doom for 'the last of the great wifettes.' For a moment Van de Graeff feels relief. There's a simple autobiographical reference here. Carraway has been married three times, always to quiet submissive women who copy-edit his final drafts while he holds forth at the Cafe Helicon chatting up the next wife in the sequence – the Bureau has a whole fat file on him.

But the final stanza brings out his night sweats. The 'laser entanglements' can only refer to those 'electric accidents' that the Bureau is so keen to talk down, those stories of 'rays' penetrating citizens at a distance, mutilating them like cattle. Only last week the Bureau had to arrange for a Radial Times reporter to be sent on a one-way assignment to the Rural territories. Yet despite all these efforts, Carraway has locked into the panic, the war-room commands – for the attack is directly beneath us, at 'six o'clock', defence is a mere suicide mission, we're already the sleep-walking dead entering the final force-field.

The room is shivering around him. The word is out, unmaking their frail civic fabrication and the City could be de-fabulated – how can he stop it now?

Mingle with the Auteurs

It's only the first interval but it has been quite a long evening already. While Igna was reading, the words seemed to slowly slide across Hermia's vision like wavy strings of white plastic lettering, in ornate fonts; and now she realises that she has only scribbled notes about the phantom typefaces, not on the poems, although at least three were sonnets celebrating the architectural wonders of the City, or so she thinks. She hopes that Esmond will not be disappointed. He has become so obsessed by his travails at the Bureau.

She looks around the ornate lobby. In the Artists' Circle she has always been at the centre, but in this crowded word-world she's an *arriviste* on the margins. Hereward Neubauer is still trying to attract the attention of Millie Honeycutt, whom he has trapped behind a marble pillar. Ibrahim F. Spruill, a recent convert to one of the Caliphatic sects, signs copies of his chapbook for one of the local dealers, nodding solemnly in his new white robes, while Igna Beth, surrounded by her entourage of fellow academics, talks intensely to her new publisher, 'suave young Morton Quimby', as they call him in the Daily Telegram. Younger members of the audience – Nirvana Lux, Rochlitz Fusilio – swagger off-set, chains on their leathers clinking. Squat bald Tybalt Turner scampers after them rummaging in a bucket. He's scattering a trail of torn and crumpled paper, only turning to gurn defiantly at the civic dignitaries as he exits.

'It's his new book *Ripping the Frazzle*. He calls it Litter-ature. You pick it up as you go along...' The voice at her shoulder is trying to be helpful. This comely black woman in a smock must be Maisie Obadiah who runs a rest-house where the artistic elite can seek refuge from the sensory overload of the City's Hospitality areas. It's supposed to be very exhausting work but Maisie is all smiles for Hermia. She smiles back, relieved to be recognised.

'Is Hilbert Carraway reading tonight?' Hermia already knows that the 'avanteer' as Esmond insists on calling him, is unlikely to be appearing in support of Igna Beth, but her husband seems especially anxious to glean any fragment of information about him.

'No, dear,' laughs Maisie. 'They tell me he's already working on a new book.'

'These younger poets – such fire! But we prefer our poems limpid, don't we? Maybe an echo of the pastoral. Especially here, in the City.'

A tannoy announces the second half. Charles Kenning will be hosting a panel on Rupert Housby-Smith and ending with some of his own verse. The women keep smiling and turn towards the auditorium.

Poetic Invention

Hilbert must not stop. He has to perform the writing, every day at eleven, on the third table from the door at the Cafe Helicon, fuelled by a sequence of herbal teas and black coffee. His skull is pressurised, new work is awaiting transcription. He sweeps aside dirty cups, opens his hefty Amiga portable and boots up Textcraft. He's ready to finger, waiting for the field to open, to hang in the indeterminate interval. The words will be clustering out there in hyperspace, in all their poly-perversity...

Flagellate all hierophants
he goes against the clockworker
all night-membranes vibrant in fatty gutters
most of you know you want to go
running out of centuries

I crawled out of quick-time
a bloody clot stopped my biogrammatics

I couldna prance the long flight paths
adding up value with a boner
to keep faith in pottaging

He falters. There's an odd sour taste in his mouth. Wincing, he writes:

Spech mus be prefect and ebonological neloglo nelo neological

A problem here. Stenographics have always been his strong point. Not like him to mis-type or back-space. He's always been able to stride the flow. He deletes the line – and looks up.

Through the window he can glimpse a figure standing on the far side of the street, motionless amid the shoppers, staring at the cafe frontage. But droplets of fresh rain are sliding down the window and a tram slowly rumbles past, so he can't see clearly for a moment. Then the watcher turns and slowly walks off in the direction of the Polyphonic Hall. But it's predictably male, in one of those black capes that the Bureau officials like to flaunt, topped by a worn anxious face with wiry glasses, a narrow face for probing and prodding. Hilbert is being observed.

How does he know? By the rupture in the flow, a sudden sick spasm in his head, the collapse of the word-function into random scrabble, whatever...Simply by watching him, focussing the intrusive institutionalised voyeurism of the Bureau at his back, this old stooge has hacked into his world-line, word-line. He's blanked. He tries another line:

speech (is) speech
always cold-calling

But it won't go any further. Now he's hyper-sensitised to the bitterness of the coffee, the drone of Astral-FM on the wireless over the bar, and the natter of three elderly women at the next table, grumbling about the incursion of yet more scruffy Rurals and rising meat prices. He's blocked. They're blocking him. The fourth time this month. Winning the Norbert Prize has made things worse, not better.

Emily, that pretty curly-haired waitress, is trying to ask him if he wants anything, some sedative cocoa perhaps – he looks so edgy this morning. Emily is solicitous, generously embodied, would make a valuable comrade, and normally he'd pursue a conversation. But it's no good. He's getting the message. He has to pack up and get out.

A Guided Walk

Hermia is spending the morning in personal development by joining a walking party on a tour of the City's more obscure cultural nodes. The group has gathered outside the Citadel. As far as she can make out, they are mostly tourists from Eurasian statelets or the Caliphatic Rim, talking in low voices under their veils and hoods as they wind up their cameras. They've probably had a dangerous journey through the Agrarian Belt Ways but they've heard so much about the City's unique psycho-demographics and now they're going to be part of it.

The guide arrives a few minutes late. She's a slim young woman with jet-black bobbed hair. There's something about the way she flicks back her forelock that's familiar – and Hermia recognises Nirvana Lux, who'd walked out on Igna's reading last night, who once fronted one of the City's most fashionable bands. Now the poetess is surviving as a mere tourist escort…Hermia wonders if she should make a note of this for Esmond, poor old Esmond who came home in the early hours and was off again at six. He told her that every detail was significant.

The group is expecting an introduction, perhaps an itinerary, but Nirvana merely points in the direction of the Imperial Marine Hotel, which is where most of them have just come from. Meekly, like a file of school children, they follow. At the side of the Hotel, Nirvana reaches into her long grey coat – no leather jacket today – and produces a forked wand of some bluish metal. She grips it with tight fists, shifting uneasily from foot to foot. Her eyes close and she grimaces. Hermia is worried. She didn't realise there were risks involved in guiding.

Then the wand trembles. Hermia even convinces herself she's glimpsing a tiny spark at its apex – she can't be sure – but Nirvana's forearms flex, twist – and then relax. She points down a cobbled alley around the side of the hotel. It leads into a maze of muddy lanes, past burnt-out workshops, sagging tin sheds and lock-ups. No one to be seen but there's a distant drunken crooning on the wind. It's starting to drizzle again. Rubble is scattered everywhere, so the visitors have to pick their way through broken half-bricks and lumps of concrete. They look hurt. Are they supposed to admire splintered crates, overturned shopping trolleys or oily pools of iridescent scum? Hermia shares their unease. The wand could be leading them astray.

The lane dips into a narrow smelly tunnel underneath Progression Avenue. Hermia, confused by the slumdog labyrinth they've just traversed, thinks they're now heading for the Hospitality District. Plenty of tourist traps there.

But the tunnel mouth opens into the overgrown lawns of a small park, clumps of rhododendrons in weedy beds, the whole bordered by high thorn bushes. They can hear the distant roar of traffic up on the embankment. Yet this little enclave seems completely cut-off from the rest of the City. There are no exit signs or gates. The way out is the way in. Hermia wonders if her husband knows of this place. It feels a very private discovery.

At the centre of the mini-park there's a paved area where Nirvana gestures for them to pause, in front of a small domed canopy on rusty iron pillars.

It houses a curious bronze statue, about two metres high. It's quasi-abstracted rather than neo-classic, stained with verdigris and pigeon droppings. A nude hermaphroditic figure, masked, holds a clutch of stylised lightning bolts in its right hand and a whip in the other. It's crowned with a clockface, with the familiar radial 'eye of lightning' motif at its centre, and wears a necklace of tiny clocks. Clocks and cocks. The phallus and breasts are pronounced. There's a slight vibration in the paving stones, a faint grinding noise. As the tourists stare and click with their whirring cameras, Hermia realises that the artefact is very slowly rotating...

One of the visitors, an elderly man in a fez, asks what it's meant to be. Nirvana looks expectantly at Hermia. She's embarrassed, she's never seen this before, but has to improvise an answer, it's the only courteous thing to do.

'I suppose – the androgyny – maybe there's a connection with the deity Baphomet – have you been to Baphomet Street yet?' The man looks blank but she continues. 'Of course, the radial motifs – that's referring to Radial City, of course. And it goes round and round. Master/mistress of all it surveys...' She laughs nervously. 'It must relate to the founding of the modern City. In fact, I think you've all seen your first Time-Tableau. Isn't that right, Nirvana?'

Nirvana ignores her and fiddles with her wand. The tourists huddle together, wondering where the current will take them next. Hermia senses that they are only at the beginning of a very long arc.

Aesthetic and Intellectual Debate

Let's roll, Rochlitz!' Tybalt Turner switches on the ancient teletype attached to his computator and adjusts its huge drum of paper. 'This is the poetry of the future!'

He presses the start button and the bulky machine starts jerking out text. Its deafening chatter makes speech impossible for a few minutes as coils of print snake across the floor.

Meanwhile Rochlitz Fusilio surveys Turner's tiny living quarters, this cunningly converted freight container in the yard of a disused glue factory just off Progression Avenue. Fusilio thinks he can still smell liquefied bones, but he's impressed by the way Tybalt has created a tiny cell for himself in the decaying body of the City's industrial zones. The bedsit space is crammed with obsolescent electronic equipment – a biogram projector, broken q-meters, an incomplete thanatron kit, boxes of old Kneale-Harrison transcenders. This anarcho-tech aspect of Tybalt is new to him. He also notices that his comrade has taped frayed sheets of rubber to the walls, supposedly a protection against the 'Rays' that old ladies whisper about. Rochlitz has an earthy pinch of Rural in his DNA and is surprised that his friend takes the urban myth so seriously. But then maybe poetry is just another form of critical paranoia…

The machine stops yammering. 'OK, let's rip and read…' Tybalt shouts, grabbing the torn sheets. 'Alternate lines, right? Say it loud. After me…'

They read:

REX ROWLEY KILLED MERVYN QUINTO/
ETHAN McCORD FUCKED MAVIS KESSLER /
JAPHET P. MORRISON BOUGHT HEIDI VUKOVITCH/
DALE DORMAN SOLD SETH PORTILLO/

REX ROWLEY FUCKED HEIDI VUKOVITCH/
ETHAN McCORD BOUGHT SETH PORTILLO
JAPHET P. MORRISON SOLD MAVIS KESSLER/
ELGIN MAHONY KILLED SOLANA SPRAGUE/

ETHAN McCORD SOLD SETH PORTILLO/
TAHIRA TYLER KILLED REX ROWLEY/

ELGIN MAHONY FUCKED JAPHET P. MORRISON/
MAVIS KESSLER BOUGHT REGINA O'DOWD/

SETH PORTILLO BOUGHT LAVORNA HEPPLETHWAITE/
MAVIS KESSLER SOLD DALE DORMAN/
JAPHET P. MORRISON FUCKED TAHIRA TYLER/
ETHAN McCORD KILLED HEIDI VUKOVITCH/

Rochlitz stops. 'There's seventy-six pages of this…What's happening, Ty?'

'This is the future sound of Radial City. Of its poetry…'

'Hilbert's stuff is the future. He led us out of Bungalow-land, he won the Norbert. He's the Indeterminator.'

'No! Listen. Hilbert and even Nirvana are trapped in the fission of the moment. Just as old Kenning and Igna the Long Pig are caught in its closure – they're pluperfect, they've had it. Meanwhile Hilbert has pushed the indeterminacy envelope as far it will go. He's put so much slippage on the signifiers that we're all gonna lose our grip. Not just the poetry crews. Once Hilbert's idiolect finds its way into copywriting or radio, the anchoring that alleged normals rely on will start corroding pretty damned quick. That's why that old goon from the Bureau is tracking him. Hilbert's amazing but – '

'Thus they in wandering mazes lost…' Rochlitz murmurs a line from nowhere, that suddenly sidled into his head.

'Absolutely! Now Hilbert dragged us young ones out of the cosy Bungalow, all Rupert's twee sonnets about civic architecture and sacred tramlines, and Kenning diddling around with his Platonic forms. But he's plunged us into an infinite labyrinth…'

Rochlitz gestures at the rumpled folds of print. 'So what's the meaning of this?'

'Back to roots, my man. A poetry of simple naming, the quiddity and unique magickal potency of the proper noun. A poetry of basic declaration – the deep structure of grammar – subject/active verb/object. A poetry stating primal needs and drives, the poetry of monosyllabic verbs – kill, fuck, buy, sell. A poetry of incessant repetition. A poetic that exposes the underlying power structures and prime activities of the City – violence, exploitation, profiteering – everything the Bureau is trying to protect. Poetry of year zero…Poetry for all!'

'Feels like a manifesto. Are you serious about this?' Rochlitz tries to sound casual, but he feels uneasy. They can't afford yet another splinter group in the poetic front – and now Tybalt's gripping his collar.

'I'm going to be the only serious poet in Radial City. I know Hilbert and Nirvana and Glotz and the others drove us into quantum shadowland, and that was a serious mission, we had to probe the sub-worlds, and that fragged the sensibilities of the Bureau. But now it's time to consolidate, get into solid matter, get some seizure in the consensus-reality with a new poetry – big, ugly, monolithic statements, in the bloody face of the Bureau interface. Meanwhile, Hilbert's still playing his fractal games…'

The container hatch screeches open. Hilbert leans through the narrow doorway, breathing heavily, clutching his text-processing pack to his chest like a life-preserver. 'You say I'm playing games? When I'm harassed by drongoids in black capes. And I'm certain they're stalking Nirvana now. A dumpy old woman on her tour this morning…'

Rochlitz has never seen their mentor so shaken. Hilbert's long hair is tangled and for the first time Rochlitz notices that the roots are greying. There's the scab of a recent skin eruption – or burn? – in the high dome of his forehead.

Tybalt stands there, hands on hips, ankle-deep in paper. 'Sorry…It's a new game now, Hilbert. Time for some full frontal…'

Uranium Cookbook

Officer Esmond Van de Graeff tries to read Nirvana Lux's *The Uranium Cookbook* propped up against the teapot while Hermia prepares their supper in the kitchenette, but the slim volume keeps falling over and Hermia has the radio turned up as usual so it's hard to concentrate. Then the lights flicker and the burble of the radio dips for a few seconds, which suggests a strategy. Perhaps if he tried reading some lines aloud he might decode the threat. Dangerous perhaps, but an Officer has to take risks.

He clears his throat:

polyps of time split into guts our lost semi-transparent friends
ticketed for the maximum blast zone they blotched into pure pain
a puritan plotted circles of radiation to rain harder
their fatlands deep-fried at the merry hub of the hubbies

Don't like the sound of that,' shouts Hermia over the hiss of boiling cabbage. 'It's horrid and un-spiritual. And quite formless. Anyway, you've got to be quiet now. The Pontiff's on in a minute.'

The Pontiff's homilies over Astral FM are a high point of Hermia's week. Today he is going to discuss *Transgression and Repentance* and really Esmond should be paying attention too, for evidence of spiritual development, tested in an annual audit, is definitely a bonus on one's Bureau employment record, but this wretched book has set something off, just as he feared, and now a dark vortex of pain is rotating inside his skull.

'...ars scribendi discitur per maleficaribus...' The Pontiff's high nasal voice is intoning something about the art of writing being taught by bad men, and Hermia is sitting mesmerised over her vegetables but Esmond can't keep up with it, can't keep up with the world.

Ongoing Pulse

Midnight and candlelight at Quibbles. Rochlitz Fusilio is finishing his final set before scattered bodies on worn sofas. His heart is pumping up the volume and he hears his voice issuing megaphonically from a point about a foot above and behind his head:

stop you berserker pixillations
who feed us the mash cabbage of attention deficit syndrome
while squirting your liquidated gold
up my colonic canyon the horizontal event
which will suck, suck harmonically your wallowing black helicopters
stop our faces in melt-down
in mid-death crystallisation or crispier flesh-pots
you can't quite get into the dream farm
with a belt of raw loins the top-hatter caper
to be destroyed by solarised beetles I have last given orders to kill
stop —

There's a commotion at the back of the room, heads turn away to see a whole entourage pushing in through the drapes at the exit. Nirvana leads them. For a second, Rochlitz hopes he's being endorsed, perhaps even discovered – and he also realises how much he's always fancied Nirvana's ivory neck and high cheekbones, always beyond the reach of his artisan hands – but she's shouting at him, at everybody…

'Tybalt's in the Fatlands! He's threatening a spectacular. There's bound to be trouble. He needs us…'

Private Sector

They gather beneath glaring orange lights, under the squat pillars of the Fatlands monorail terminal. The dark pods of the cylindrical cars hang over them, like fat bombs, yet to be tested.

Most of the pottage-bars are closed, but thick odours on the night wind suggest that the labs of the Organ Exchange are still processing today's tissue-harvests. A sewage man trundles quietly past in his electric cart.

As Nirvana's crew side-steps a sleepy security guard and takes a short cut through the high atrium of the Money Exchange, the screens are blinking non-stop in kiosks and work-stations. One or two traders stare irritably at this gaggle of rag-bag chancers, but most are too absorbed in the creation of virtual capital to take any notice of the brief intrusion. They exit quickly into the Central Plaza.

'Why is he performing here and now? This zone is monitored 24/7. They'll march him off in five minutes…' Rochlitz points to the hoods of the Bureau security detectors high on the balconies. Their footsteps echo down the long vistas of concrete and black glass.

Nirvana sighs. Big ox-faced Rochlitz has always been so literal-minded. 'He's going for the solar plexus, the belly of the City. A psychic stake through the stake-holders!' She pulls out her metal wand and staggers slightly on one foot. 'Can't you feel it?'

Now even Rochlitz can feel a faint chakric trickle in his spinal column. She must be aligning them to a current that will steer them to Tybalt's mysterious point of convergence. Perhaps Tybalt has followed an older time-track, embedded long before the erection of the Fatlands. Or maybe it's a warning, a spasm induced by those civic myths, the Rays…

Another group, clustered around an excitable Glotz, merges with them as they pass the foetid water feature outside the Zelazowski Brothers building. Some of the newcomers are carrying hastily painted banners. One reads:

THE POETS HAVE GONE ALL AARDVARK.

Then, at the base of the Bournegate Complex – a thirty-storey pyramid of smoked glass and weathered bronzite – Rochlitz sees the blue flicker of police warning lights and the silhouette of heavy-duty half-tracks, their fluid cannons angled towards the upper floors. As he predicted there's a line of helmeted riot police, probably toughs recruited from the Rural belt. 'It looks bad,' he mutters, but Nirvana ignores him, too deeply engrossed with Hilbert, who has just joined them. Hilbert points to an elderly man in a cape standing awkwardly beside a Bureau truck, clutching a loudhailer as if uncertain of its function. 'Is that supposed to be their so-called negotiator? That old beak who keeps stalking me?'

Searchlights strafe the north face of the building. Rochlitz looks up. On a narrow terrace close to the apex, a small figure is caught in the cross-beams. Tybalt is hunched over a conglomeration of his electronic junk. Somehow he has abseiled with this kit up the sixty degree slope of the structure, spidering his way along the metal interstices between the glossy panels and facades.

That elderly man now grips his megaphone and bellows. But his tinny syllables reverb into garble. Tybalt yells back, a rhythmic yell, with a familiar pattern of structure and stress:

SETH PORTILLO BOUGHT LAVORNA HEPPLETHWAITE/
MAVIS KESSLER SOLD DALE DORMAN/
JAPHET P. MORRISON FUCKED TAHIRA TYLER/
ETHAN McCORD KILLED HEIDI VUKOVITCH/

Rochlitz automatically joins in, mouthing the antiphonal responses. Nirvana stares but Hilbert has begun swaying back and forth, stomping to the beat. Rochlitz starts a new cycle.:

TAHIRA TYLER BOUGHT ODYSSEUS OGDEN/
JACKLYN BORKLAND SOLD LENNARD R. DRISCOLL/
WALLIS X. TAGGART FUCKED TINA-LEIGH KLEINDORFER/
ALEX VON HUFHAUSEN KILLED JOE BORZILLO

Twisting away to glance at the opposite tower, Dworkin Funds, Nirvana notes flickers, flecks of light across the black panes. They're forming strings of letters. Is Tybalt projecting these scrawls of light, an emanation from his techno-trash hi-rise installation?

Now text is crawling across the portico of the Radial Central Bank. Letters squirm and loop like melting neon – magenta morphing into purple, lime-green, orange, burning gold. It is a long looping spiel of naming:

SETH PORTILLO KILLED LAVORNA HEPPLETHWAITE/
MAVIS KESSLER SOLD DALE DORMAN/
ODYSSEUS OGDEN FUCKED TINA-LEIGH KLEINDORFER/
ETHAN McCORD BOUGHT SETH PORTILLO

MAVIS KESSLER SOLD LAVORNA HEPPLETHWAITE/
ELGIN MAHONY KILLED SOLANA SPRAGUE/
DALE DORMAN FUCKED ETHAN McCORD/
ALEX VON HUFHAUSEN BOUGHT JACKLYN BORKLAND/

The signifiers swing across the chasms between the towers, revolving, dissolving, deforming, reforming into warped cones, malformed helices, disintegrating spirals and luminous tendrils of warped glyphs. But they're passing sentences. They name names, all those names scrolling down the City's walls of glass…

Cultural Industries

Hermia Van de Graeff checks the clock. She can't sleep. Esmond has been called out again – at his age, at this time of night – to deal with some trouble in the financial district. Surely that Quarmby woman is deliberately persecuting him. But he won't talk, just hides in his den or reads out those odd poems in a low anxious voice.

For the third time, she turns off the bedside lamp. But she leaves Astral FM on, very low. Jack Hague's phone-in comforts her with its faint plaintive buzz of indignation. A man is mumbling about garbage collection schedules. Quite right too. She slides into vague reverie. She must be dreaming.

She's in the Fatlands. The high towers seem oddly skewed. And they're decorated, as if for some winter festivity, switched on too early, surely? They're adorned with strings of illuminated letters, glittering alphabets, which flash across the chasms. They're spellbinding, spelling out names, proper names, names she almost recognises, that she must have seen or maybe heard on the radio. She looks for Esmond's name. He must be in there somewhere...

Suddenly people are swarming out of their lobbies, atriums, boardrooms, running and stumbling frantically as if in response to a fire-alarm, a bomb alert. Or a roll-call.

They mill around the wide precinct opposite Beaverdale Securities, except it's been renamed Fatlands House and the ornamental fountains spout gouts of flame like burning oil rigs. Her eyes are flying. She pans and zooms through high G contortions trying to follow their action plan.

One cluster of suits seems to be setting up an open-air market like a Rurals market, except these aren't Rurals, they're Neural traders to judge from their white-trimmed hats. The stall is an overturned boardroom table. Everyone's starting to shout and wave bits of paper which she recognises as money. No security guards around, so nasty things are going on, she's just seen an attractive brunette, thirties, a junior manager in her brown skirt, manhandled on to an upturned crate, with a scrum of trainee Fatlanders tearing her blouse as they squabble over her, until a distinguished-looking silver haired man with a machete starts hacking away at their limbs until their blood runs glistening under the floodlights...

She must find Esmond.

She's woken by the distant wail of sirens and the throb of gyrocopters; and starts sobbing.

Epicentre

Tybalt can barely hear the old man with the loudhailer as the mobs seethe and sway below. They're roaring their brand names and acting out their sentences. He can see pyres burning throughout the precincts and the screaming has started, merging into a mush of red noise. He never expected this release of energy. He is Dionysus; but this is a negative ecstasy, vertiginous, a nausea of pure terror. He repeats an internalised strapline, his tag: *We are all terrorists now.*

127

Now the man with the loudhailer is submerged by the crowd swarming around his truck. Up here with Tybalt the scenario is all remote, the vehicle is miniaturised. Yet he can see they're going to rock it over, roll it all over the trained negotiator, who's in the bloody Fatlands now, they've turned on him, loyal servant of the Bureau. He disappears in a hideous scrum of fists and broken glass as the managerial classes execute their human resources policy and meet their new target.

Suddenly Tybalt's left eye stings unbearably and blacks out. Those Bureau police must be using lasers. He can hear his scream rising over the uproaring. He staggers on the ledge of the terrace, half-blinded – and then stumbles/tumbles with increasing velocity down the sixty degree slope of the pyramid, accelerating too fast to locate handholds with his bloodied fingers, rolling over the inclined planes of black glass to bounce from terrace to terrace, crashing down the ziggurat to thud on the asphalt. An end-line flickers through his terminal pain:

SERENA QUARMBY KILLED TYBALT TURNER

Heritage

Hermia sits in Esmond's den, gazing at the muddle of his scrapbooks, faded circuit diagrams for his unfinished inventions, those teetering heaps of poetry magazines with cryptic annotations. She is benumbed.

Dr Morphy has sent a cyclostyled letter of condolence and a form that will allow her to apply for a widow's pension. The Bureau will, of course, hold an enquiry into the circumstances surrounding her husband's demise, although many of those named as participants are themselves dead or unavailable. Many colleagues, in full uniform, led by Serena Quarmby, attended at the City crematorium, which left Hermia feeling oddly estranged, almost an observer at a corporate team-bonding exercise. But dear Charles Kenning was charming, although she gently refused his offer of a funeral address. There have been too many words. She wanted a long silence before the coffin rolled away behind the jerky curtains.

State of the Art

The poets huddle under the canopy over the revolving statue in the small park near Progression Avenue. It's raining heavily. Nearby Rochlitz and

Hilbert have dug a muddy grave. Nirvana is red-eyed, quivering under a twisted umbrella. Maisie Obadiah comforts her and hands out hot soup. A dozen gather around Rochlitz as he reads:

THE POETS have an additive of voices that fill space. The posse uses an abandoned database in the Language Zone.
This battle field is actioned, a classified field, their Area 93 of wire fences and dogshit spirals, but they keep trudging through trying to sing their song...

Above them, in the heavy clouds, the radiance of the City flickers.

Hours of Darkness

– Tessa West –

She set off at ten. Just past the traffic lights she crossed over, turned left into a small road and decided to follow it to the next junction. She knew he wouldn't be far away.

She walked between a long line of parked cars and tiny front gardens behind low walls. Incompletely pulled curtains framed glimpses of a woman holding a baby, a man with his head in his hands, a screen showing soldiers advancing across a white desert.

At first she didn't realise he was a person. He looked like a pile of earth or leaves heaped up against some steps and it was difficult to make him out because one of the street lights was not working. He was lying face down, one knee loosely pulled towards his chest. His arms were spread out like dislocated wings, his head turned to the side. He had fallen just as a victim hit on the head is supposed to fall, ready for someone to draw round in chalk so the position remains marked on the ground after the body has been taken to the morgue.

She looked down at him, then along the length of the street. They were alone. A small noise came from his half-open mouth. A tiny muttering. She knelt beside him and saw his closed, dark eyelids, the hair in his nostrils, his swollen lip. Blood moved from his mouth like a thin stream of cooling lava.

The drizzle was making her damp, and the cold rose up from her knees into her legs, her thighs. She reached out to touch him. She stroked the veins on the back of his hand, pulled down his cuff and loosened his collar. Yellow headlights swept over them but the driver did not stop. She stayed still on the pavement. A burst of canned laughter reached her from some distant place. Now the blood had stopped moving but there was another slight sigh, a small exhalation that she felt through his fingers. Then a door opposite opened, a voice said goodbye, and the door closed. Footsteps went the other way, towards the lights. Relieved, she touched his head. His thick hair did not yet know that he was on the cusp of death. She shifted her position in preparation for the night. She would wait with him, watch over him. She would stay with him until the next day came, before natural light returned. By then these creases in his neck, these shallow hollows between the bones of his wrists, these knuckles of his hand would be familiar. By the time the next day came to life she would know this man. There would be time.

An hour passed and a few cars went by, all going in the same direction, all shining their lights on the wet road and the place where she was sitting. A woman unpadlocked a bike from some railings and rode off. Two men passed on the opposite pavement, their shoes sending up drops of recent rain. She moved herself onto the corner of the man's open jacket to be close to him, but it did not protect her from the cold and wet. This did not matter. Already, her body was almost as numb as his. His faltering pulse held promise.

She felt filled with a patient energy. Already she knew the curve of his spine, the way his top teeth – one of them slightly chipped – were just visible under the edge of his upper lip, the way new growth would emerge slowly from his slack chin. She was beginning to piece him together. She knew it worked best if she concentrated on one part of his body and then shut her eyes for a few minutes. When she looked back she'd discover another part of him. Just now she'd found the ridge of his collar-bone linking his shoulder to his neck. This pleased her. She liked too the fact that one leg was extended and stretched out with the knee and foot on the ground. The upturned wet heel and sole of his shoe reflected light, sent out weak beams at the edge of her focus. The other leg was bent and his thin black trousers had rucked up, leaving a gap that drew her eyes to his pale ankle. She resisted the desire to cover it with her scarf.

When the pub at the end of the road closed a group of young people emerged. She was not expecting this and tensed up until they went off the other way. While this was happening she failed, unusually for her, to notice a couple approaching from behind. Hand-in-hand and engrossed in conversation they stepped off the kerb to avoid what they thought was a pile of rubbish. She welcomed this evidence that she and the man were almost invisible.

Night set in properly. Though she heard traffic in other streets, no-one else walked or drove past the two of them. Lights went out downstairs, upstairs. She was still, he was still. It seemed to her that progress was gradually being made. Studying the bulk of his body she realised how solidly he was built. Although this meant it might take longer, there was plenty of time. The more she thought about his body, the less she was conscious of her own.

Soon it was time to start talking. She was sure he was ready by now. She began to describe the surroundings. She did this so that he became used to her and prepared for what was to come. He lay and listened, altering his position slightly.

Then she asked, 'How has life led you here? Who are you?'

He began, as they all did, to hesitate, then start and stop again. 'It's difficult to explain,' he said, as they all did.

She waited, knowing that he would continue, and he continued. He told her about the house he'd grown up in, his parents, the sister who had died, his studies, his marriage to a woman who made him feel guilty, his two daughters, the interest yet dissatisfaction of his work, his garden with its corner of privacy and sunlight, his weekday routine, his walk home from the bus, the blow he'd been dealt.

'Who are you?' she asked again.

'How can I answer? I cannot answer.'

'Tell me who you are,' she said, gently.

'I am...I don't know. I can't remember my name. There are things I don't want to remember. I was jealous when my sister died and my parents forgot me in their grief for her, and I can't forgive them, but I know too that I might behave as they did if one of my daughters were to die. I cannot understand how I have forgotten my name.'

'Your name does not matter now.'

'If I have no name, then I am who I am. An injured man lying on a pavement.'

'Good. Yes. You are who you are. A man lying on a pavement, but a man with a history.'

'But I have no future.'

'You have a future.'

'How can I have a future?'

'Because the future will not be stopped. You will be part of it. The blow to your head was the beginning. It is your opportunity.'

'What does my future hold?'

'Be patient for a few hours and it will be upon you. It will arrive.'

'But will my life be the same as before?'

'That depends on you. Do you want to be the same? You can change.'

'I tell myself I am doing my best but I know it is not good enough. I do not love my wife enough. And because of this I do not give all of myself. How should I change this?'

'That's up to you. I cannot say. But you have a choice about who to be and how to be.'

'What should I do?'

'It's up to you. It will always be up to you.'

He did not reply, and, with the reluctance which she experienced each time she started this conversation, she let him retreat from the foreground and become part of the wider scene.

The night took its course.

Although she had not heard the clock before, she heard it strike three. Then a dustbin lid clattered to the ground and a thin gingery fox jumped onto a wall. It stood and looked at her intently. Suddenly, urgently, she wanted him to see the fox too, so she leaned forward and touched his closed eyes. She felt his precious round eyeballs just beneath the fragile skin. This spontaneous gesture was the most intimate one she had made that night and for a few moments her heartbeat accelerated. Raising her head she saw that the fox had gone. Now she had to concentrate on what had to be done next.

She placed her outstretched hands on his back and started to murmur slowly. Then she began to hum a low tune as she pressed her palms firmly against his shoulder blades. She knew he would not be able to resist. Not a single one of them had been able to resist. After an hour she could feel a slight warmth coming through his jacket. As she shifted her soft song to a different key she noticed a small movement of his leg, a change in the angle of his knee. Gradually he responded. She took her time, working her way from the small of his back down across the damp fabric covering his buttocks, his thighs, his legs, and then up to his shoulders, his arms and their lean biceps, his elbows, his hands. Scarcely perceptible thin vapour rose from his mouth as she hummed a single, continuous note.

Unable to prevent herself she tenderly lifted her hand, turned it over and studied the inside of his wrist. Then, against the rules she had set herself but often struggled to obey, she slowly bent her head to kiss the small area of skin that was beginning to flutter like a fontanelle. She replaced his hand and turned to his face. Faces were difficult because they would suddenly come into being and alive under her touch. Grief surfaced in her as he began to breathe and return to his body. He made the small involuntary shudder that new-born babies make.

She was crooning under her breath as she covered his face with her hands, then put careful pressure on his cheeks, forehead, nose, the line of his jaw, the place where his hair was beginning to recede. She was witnessing his arrival, and this saddened her because it signalled his departure. She had wanted to learn him, to know him, and she had done so. When she heard the first sound from a bird she knew it was time to go.

He was wiping his mouth now, struggling to sit up. She moved away from him, denying the urge to put the finishing touches to his earlobes, his bruised temple.

The morning was underway. Traffic increased, people were on the move. As noise entered the street the lights went out, leaving a streaked sky to take over. He was on his feet now, rubbing his eyes as he leaned against a wall in his crumpled clothes. He looked dazed, amazed. She observed him with satisfaction.

Stations of the Cross

– Ian Madden –

Long past midnight and Christopher Staunch is sitting at his kitchen table staring at four cardboard bow ties – all maroon – and mulling over the errand that had spurred him out earlier in the evening.

Licking a thumbnail discoloured by powdered thyme, it's not the herb he can taste so much as the pastry in which it had been wrapped.

Outside the wind is still raging; pushing at doors, knocking over plant pots, flinging milk shake cartons with drinking straws still in them into the sky and away.

There is no overhead lighting in his house. (Not his house exactly but the compound dwelling assigned to him by the company when he came to work in the Sultanate). He long since removed all the bulbs from the ceiling fittings and bought table lamps for every room. In the kitchen at night the only illumination is from the underside of the wall units. He finds it calming.

Equipped with plates, pots, copper-bottomed pans and an implement not even a neighbour who enjoyed cooking could identify ('I think it's a rolling pin for garlic...') the kitchen provides a pleasing prospect of tasks he knows he'll never attempt. In the muted light, hope will not leave him alone. There it is once again, shameless as ever, saliva swinging off its chin. For the second consecutive night he doesn't feel like going to bed.

This time last night he was inspecting jeans soiled at the knee, a bruise starting where he stumbled. And as a result of seeking a reprise of it, this evening left his fingers crimson and stinging from coat hanger hooks.

If the weather hadn't turned nasty would he have kept returning to that Moorish café every hour or so to sit and eat pastries – and pretend not to be keeping a lookout?

It had taken a sandstorm to make him see sense.

To those who don't share his interests let alone his obsession, what he's pondering may as well be a story told by someone in waders standing mid-stream, a snap-lid container full of writhing maggots on the riverbank behind him; or tottering on a makeshift dais, demented in a sequined gown, miming to a histrionic torch song. Shorn of all other attributes, anyone proclaiming this particular interest must sound shallow or trashy. But its claim is just as strong as its worthier counterparts. Staunch wanted to enumerate – to whom? – a long and worthy list of his other traits, not just this craving.

Surely there must be more to impart than a stealthy climb, a tussle on a rooftop and the rancorous doubt that his preoccupation comes off worse qualitatively when set beside those deemed more mentionable.

What's the point of experience if all you do is hope for exceptions to the lessons it has taught? This shrillness soon mellows into at least you tried.

Hope, moderated by the view from the Way of Sorrows, could still soar.

Who hasn't made a fool of himself yearning over beauty or thuggishness? And who hasn't gone overboard at the idea of blissful togetherness? Snuggled beside an inglenook fireplace for ever and ever. Unless you're unfortunate these blemishes, like the pimples of pubescence, clear up. Despite his hard-won grown-upness, his self-control broke out in a gawky adolescent rash late on Monday night. Sand, gritty on his back teeth, is a reminder of the moment that evening he had given up. Or given up for now. *I should have known better.* He *did* know better. That was just it...

The air in the lobby was dense from all the incense that had been wafted in preparation for the ruler. The Sultan of Fawan himself was due to officially open the new complex bearing his name. Surrounded by courtiers all of whom seemed to believe that their boss was three parts deity, the object of their veneration was made way for. Looking every bit as obese, shiny and corrupt as the brother he ousted fifteen or so years earlier, the stocky potentate walked surprisingly nimbly along the scented corridor.

Monday has the feel of a Wednesday in the Sultanate; it being the third day of the working week. Whenever Staunch makes the trip downtown, he's usually home by eleven. But yesterday he'd had to go back to the company's offices in the evening to sit through the opening ceremony. Every member of the department Staunch worked in had been dragooned into attending lest the sight of an empty seat in the auditorium affront the sultan's gaze. Returning to work after an eight-hour day and in what should have been their free time was an act of endurance. The enforced courtesies, the craven inclines of the head, the standing around looking interested, the numbing speeches; all were wearying. What got Staunch through was the thought of the reward he hoped would be his later that night.

Employees were offered a little bottle of water ('sterilized by ozone') for coming – but which could not be taken into the auditorium. At one point in the ceremony the sultan sat and received praise from a young man standing behind a lectern who ranted at him as if pleading for his life.

Staunch wondered how long all this would go on for and whether he'd be allowed out to go to the lavatory. In full view of the sultan he got up, went down the steps and along to the nearest exit. Perhaps – because he wasn't a citizen of the Sultanate – Staunch was granted a fool's pardon by the guard and was let out. After a leisurely visit to the toilet he returned to the exit he had come out of. The same guard would not readmit him. Nor could Staunch – when he tried – leave the building. So he went to sit in the corridor near one of the tables from which the bottled water had been handed out.

Hours later, when the royal motorcade finally left, Staunch caught a taxi downtown where he ate a large salad and a small steak. With that appetite sated, he bought a few articles at a nearby grocery. Best not to be empty-handed. Then he set about looking for opportunities to sate the other appetite. With not long to go before the shops were to shut, he wandered over to a shopping precinct where, on some weeknights, the security guards outnumbered the shoppers. At the side entrance, on the pavement in front of the toy kiosk, the usual wayward regiment of battery-powered playthings whizzed, swayed and bleeped. Sidestepping a chubby shuffling gorilla as it weakly attempted to clash cymbals, Staunch went round to the loading bay at the rear. Its bulging black plastic bags, stacks of cardboard packaging, its stinks; all were preferable to the ersatz air and the vigilance – both human and mechanical – inside. Beyond the heaps of refuse, not quite in and not quite out of the building, was a corridor. At its far end were two glass doors through which several shops – a bedding supplies shop, a place which sold reproductions of paintings (mostly of ancient stone portals) and another whose window contained the message 'We Care For Your Good Taste' and whose wares he had yet to discover – could be seen. Staunch did not go as far as the shops. The door he wanted was closer to the loading bay, first on the left.

Forearms outstretched on the pine table, Staunch sighs and picks up the laundry bow ties. He holds them between the thumb and forefinger of each hand, splayed, as though they are his hand in a game of poker. If only, he thinks, there were indeed tactics which could be employed to manoeuvre one's way off a particular, seemingly personal Dolorosa.

Last night sleep had been ruled out by amazement and gradual thankfulness at what had not presented itself to block or ruin the encounter. It had gone so smoothly. One exception after another. A series of connected absences had, he now sees, worked in their favour. All it would have taken for him to lose nerve would have been a worker dawdling in the final street or a car trawling past at the wrong moment. That didn't happen. They went to where they were going. They hadn't been disturbed. And the thing to which Staunch had paid nuzzling obeisance had been distinctive, memorable. Also, thought Staunch, *he'd* seen *me*; *he'd* led *me* somewhere. Most unbelievable of all, the man in the doorway had been on foot.

Even though it was chilly February the men's room was fetid. The doors of all four lock-ups were open. Not a thing. Not so much as an automatic flush to enliven the urinal pots. The only activity was the clanking made by an overalled attendant with bucket and mop on a trolley outside.

To get from the shopping centre over to where the action is – or sometimes can be – six lanes of traffic had to be crossed. The three southbound lanes were separated from the rest by a strip the width of two paving slabs. A line of palm trees ran down the middle of this stretch. On reaching it he had to duck the fronds as he tried to see if there was anything approaching from the other direction. Many drivers used this straight drag to reassert themselves after the insult to their manhood of having had to stop at a red light. When there was a momentary gap in the traffic, Staunch stepped out from behind the fronds and sauntered across the remaining lanes; his walk so unhurried as to be provocative. The kerb to which he made his way – itself a stride high – had four or five steps which led to a raised walkway housing a row of big-windowed shops selling – among other things – plaited breads, gym equipment and clingy clothes for adult males with schoolboy hips.

Virtually every thoroughfare in the Sultanate was named after some ancestor, brother or son of the present ruler. Being shiny and splendid, this stretch doubtless was too. The shop fronts above the eye level of drivers were pristine and somehow snooty; as if having to look up at them were an indication of their prestige. But there were more important reasons why passing drivers might look up.

The streets behind the elevated shops were quieter, less populous. Over the past few weeks, encounters in this haphazard grid had amounted to no more than Staunch putting his hand over the wound-down window of an obliging car and having a leisurely squeeze of a pliant crotch. Unlike some foot-soldiers, Staunch will not get into the first vehicle that sidles up to him. Going for a ride with someone sight unseen, (or feel unfelt) was for those of a more speculative nature.

If watchfulness was necessary in England where all he risked was a warning, arrest, court appearance or fine, how much more necessary it was in this city, this country. Getting what he was looking for could cost him his life. So he varied his routes, hardly ever walking all the way along the lit street or all the way along its unlit counterpart. Instinct and hunch as much as anecdotal evidence helped formulate the rules (maybe highly personal, maybe universal) by which he must abide.

A Fawani medical student who once took Staunch back to his apartment casually told him that the secret police sometimes keep watch from further up the street in which they'd struck up a conversation.

'How do you know?'

'He sits in an old white coupe a couple of blocks down from the Chinese restaurant.'

'What does he do?'

'Nothing. That's how you can tell what he is. He never gets out. He just sits. And the car never moves.'

If familiarity had neutralised the designers' names above the windows facing the better-lit side of the street then round the back the names of those still clambering retained their outlandishness. The harsh light flung out by the first of these clinical interiors made him squint. After walking in a straight line for three or four buildings and nothing in view, Staunch decided to go back to the more public side of the avenue. There, on weeknights after the final prayer and for most of the evening at weekends, the brazen and the brave perch on or stand near the small wall along the edge of the wide pavement, actively waiting. No one was loitering now.

Cars sped by in what – from the walkway – seemed a sunken rut. This strip always gave Staunch the feeling of being open to inspection, as on a catwalk. Before he got very far along it, a hulking vehicle – painted the darkest shade of desert camouflage – slowed down as it approached. From what was on show of the driver, he looked broad and swarthy. Fist propped against his cheek and driving with one hand, he pulled over and beckoned, without taking his fist from his cheek. Staunch went through a gap in the low wall and blundered down the steps. In his haste he missed the last one, slid, fell forward. He held out his hands. His palms stung as they hit the dusty door.

'Hello.' They spoke at the same time.

Slowly, the driver took his knuckles from his face. The cheek on which he had been resting his fist looked like it had been frozen by Novocain. Again he gestured for Staunch to join him.

Opposite them were high buildings, the reflective panes of which could serve as vantage points. Staunch never suspended his caution. Any time not as nerve-ridden as the first could very well be the last.

'I'll meet you in the next street, at the back of these shops. I'll walk. You drive. We can go somewhere.'

The driver nodded.

Limping slightly, Staunch took a short cut from the over-lit avenue to the barely lit backstreet which ran parallel to it. Determined to make up for his clumsiness on the steps with the unfaltering precision with which he would have the man out of that bulky piece of army surplus and through the entrance of a deserted commercial building and up the stairs, Staunch waited beside a skip around which three or four bony cats were scavenging. The sharp-shouldered creatures tore at bags of refuse with their teeth. Sensing a threatening presence, they stopped in mid-rip. Sighting Staunch, each creature made wary estimations then cautiously resumed their task.

He hadn't been watching the cats for very long when the military-looking machine lumbered back into view. It pulled over. The driver jumped out, closed the door and walked towards Staunch. The driver was even broader than he had seemed when sitting, and taller. In dark fawn fatigues and t-shirt, he moved with that straight-backed languor common in the Gulf. A couple of seconds and they'd be through the entrance doors and waiting for the lift to take them to the top floor where there is an unused staircase which leads to a door which leads to the roof. The door is always locked.

A familiar car swerved up alongside them. It was a dark blue Caprice Classic. It looked like a flock of savage beaks had tried to peck its roof open. This car came to a stop outside the building into which Staunch was about to lead the man in fatigues. Gesticulating and leering to the point where Staunch would've liked to hit him with something, the stalwart remained Caprice-bound.

As if to test the limits of his disbelief another car of the same model – white this time, and almost as weathered – drove past, slowed, reversed, then parked in front of the blue nuisance. The unknown driver was as hintproof as the one Staunch recognized. This one seemed to believe that all he'd have to do to turn a Westerner to putty was clench his piratical teeth and make his eyebrows do a jig.

There goes a session behind the top-floor lift shaft, Staunch thought. The quest now changed from finding a place where they wouldn't be disturbed to shaking off this pest. Still on the upper level of pavement, the road several steps beneath, Staunch ambles towards the spot from which the secret policeman is said to keep watch.

No old white coupe tonight.

Staunch took a careful look over his shoulder. The man in fatigues had vanished. So had the car with the pecked roof. This was only to be expected. Fawanis do not like other Fawanis to know they do this sort of thing. The leerer in the white car was obviously too bird-brained to care. The white car glided past and came to an insolent stop outside the Chinese restaurant. On that corner the footways were covered with bright, artificial turf. Staunch descended the emerald-bristled steps in plodding dressage motion. Then he stood by the white car; behind him a sinister sizzling from the strip of red light which outlined the pagoda fins of the restaurant. Staunch took a deep breath as if he was about to resume an argument or explain patiently. His stance, for anyone who could read, read: *This had better be good.*

On the table beside the bow ties is a roll of kitchen towels, a bag of sugar – the sugar from last night – not yet deposited in the plastic carrier dangling from the door handle. This method of storage had started the previous summer when Staunch returned from the long break to find every surface in the kitchen overrun with ants. Sugar played host to the highest concentration of the insects. Scrubbing, swabbing and winter had seen them off but the precaution remained.

Staunch could, he supposes, go into the next room and lounge on one of those two nearly wall-length sofas. Sitting upright at a table he can better feel numb and nostalgic for something that happened – he glances at the kitchen clock – just over twenty-four hours ago. It's as if this expectant position will throw up more answers than if he fully relaxed.

Yes, yes, yes, it should be possible to anticipate how these things end. But hope gets in the way. Granted, it's a familiar path. But the footsteps are new – are *now* – so, despite what the landmines of experience teach there is always a thrill when the present throws a punch and knocks insensate its more cautious rival. *Expect* is the word on the victor's lips.

The troglodyte dip of the chin was perfunctory: at once invitation and imperative. Idiotically expectant, the man started to grope himself. After a quick look over his shoulder, he lifted his long white shirt and began massaging between his legs. Both car and underwear were dyed a sickly pink by the neon. The man stroked, rubbed and pulled at the material.

Staunch remained where he was; not out of interest but because moving off again could have made this one – the one he didn't want – resume the chase. If Staunch was to get into this man's car he'd need a compelling reason. The man's hand slid down inside his underwear but Staunch wasn't convinced that the area being kneaded was all (or even partially) genitalia. That the performance Staunch was watching did not include lopping it out – however briefly – invited a swift conclusion.

So, in retaliation for the manner of his arrival but mainly because Staunch wanted to prove him wrong – the leerer *was* resistible – Staunch walked round the bonnet of the car and off toward the main street. Which – praise be – was one-way. Walking against the direction of the traffic gave Staunch the advantage. If the leerer was intent on further pursuit he'd have to do what was all but unthinkable for most Fawani men. He'd have to get out of his car and walk.

By then it was past eleven. The intersection looked bare. Staunch crossed the road and went up white marble steps to the ledge of pavement which comprised the corner of the haughtiest block in that part of town. Two reflections were offered in the august window of the Specialized Cloaks Dealer; the first was what any full-length pane of glass will tell you. Immediately behind that was a less unforgiving image, muted by gilded Venetian blinds.

148

A glance behind him showed that the groper had given up.

In a parking bay in front of the jewelers, the big-wheeled machine and its broad driver waited. Pleased that his movements had been anticipated, Staunch went up to the vehicle and opened the door. The driver made the same motion for him to get in.

'It's getting late. Another time,' Staunch said.

What is it about uncomplicated willingness that makes me back off?

They exchanged names and numbers. Staunch said he would phone him soon. Further along the street, after the man had driven off, Staunch hailed a taxi. The driver was Pakistani. He wore a grubby prayer cap and his beard was dyed red. When told the destination, the driver asked for a fare double the usual. Staunch could've stayed to haggle but he didn't. He closed the door and walked on. Another taxi slowed down. Its driver asked for a fare that was usually the last resort in the bartering for that distance. But Staunch was less interested in going home than he was in the figure in black loitering by the darkened window of the party supplies shop – and obviously watching him in its reflection.

The silver structure over the oven range looks impressive – ecclesiastic, even – in the subdued light. But it seems to be three or four sizes too big. Perhaps this one (what are they *called?*) had been fitted by mistake. Dignified, it seems to await a function less mundane than the drawing away of cooking odours.

Utensils hang mysterious in a line against the far wall, catching some of the sparse light. They seemed, when he first saw them, to challenge Staunch to find out what their intended purposes were. They spoke – and still speak – of the amount of time some people dedicate to preparing food. Those who know what they are for and who use them regularly must spend as much time making meals as Staunch does in his chosen pursuit. The continued mystery of their shapes and purposes reassure him.

The wind is a reassurance, too.

'My friend...' the figure moved away from the shop window and went to stand in the recessed doorway of an office building.

Dressed in black ankle-length shirt and white head-dress, the youth was in his early twenties and had a timeless face, a face that would one day belong to a water-pipe-puffing old man. But as it was, with wrinkles yet to be earned, he had the features seen on the cover of guidebooks;

satisfied with simplicities, eyes amused that his commonplaces should be of such interest to outsiders.

Staunch approached. The young man offered no handshake or greeting just a rapid rattle of English words: Room, Sex, Good, Number One, Hotel and Fuck.

'Do you live in the city?' Staunch asked.

Either the youth didn't understand or was too wound up in his spiel – or both. He merely repeated the same desperate words but in a different order.

'No room,' Staunch said. 'Problem.'

On the wall, over the nervy shoulder was a board, black with little holes in, which listed – in detachable white lettering – the firms on every floor. No company's function was readily explicable. Staunch reached between the young man's legs. Yet more buckshot of individual words was punctuated by a brief kiss on Staunch's lips. The youth indicated going upstairs and stepped onto the black rubber mat which should have activated the double doors. When they remained closed, he urged, 'Okay, side, side.'

'You go. I'll follow.'

The eyes doubted this. They suspected larceny.

The sound made by the Arab's long garment as it got caught and released in the haste of his walk was panicky yet authoritative. Keeping him in the peripheral vision with which he had first spotted the man Staunch looked in various shop windows. The youth, his whole body alert, marched along the stretch of windows and entrances until he reached the luxury confectioner's on the corner. The low cement wall outside the shop was usually occupied by drivers and chaperones of the women visiting the coffee shop at which men are forbidden. The shop was closed, the wall unoccupied.

To their right, cars, neither prying nor relevant, were slowing down before the lights at the junction. The glimmer of a Moorish café looked distant through the hedge which separated the traffic lanes. The youth turned left, walked past the confectioner's wall and carried on down the dark street.

Under his breath Staunch began bargaining with something or someone: I've had my fair share of obstructions and obtuseness for one night. Don't let there be an aimless straggler standing in the vicinity of wherever I'm being led. He felt a sudden spasm of anger at someone as yet unspotted but already hated; the oblivious by-stander whose casualness – mighty and undirected – may as well have been deliberate spite, such was its triumphant effect: thwarting the sex plans of others.

The figure in black hurried down the middle of the road, his sandaled stride agitated and distrustful. Every few seconds he looked over his shoulder. The desperate haste made Staunch think of an illustration from a cautionary childhood tale showing a miser embracing a treasure chest bulging with coins, thinking up measures to keep what was his from being taken from him. It was primeval the way the man kept checking; was his quarry following, was every one of those pieces of eight still there?

They were in a street so empty it made Staunch doubt his luck and suspect his senses. From behind a row of darkened delivery vans, he kept the youth in his sights. Staunch found it difficult to keep his balance, walking on a sliver of kerb – there was no pavement, just kerb. The muted, purposeful swipe and thrash of the long black shirt against the man's shins was, to Staunch, promise and threat in equal measure. Then the Arab dodged through a doorway. The building Staunch followed him into was squat, box-like – a block of flats? Having stopped, turned round, he gathered his black garment to his knees and took the stairs three at a time.

Again, no people.

On the top floor were two doors: one open, one closed. The closed door was brown and had a name in English on it. Staunch could do no more than register that they were letters from the alphabet: he had neither the breath nor the composure to put them together. The open door led onto the roof. They went through this door together. By the frosted window of the rooftop flat, a row of t-shirts and socks hung on a washing line. Behind the window, a light was on. After the deft way he'd been led there, it startled Staunch when his guide was incautious enough to stand in front of this lighted pane. In his urgency – doubloons, doubloons! – nothing was allowed to impede the young man's purpose; not even the high, dark office block across the street. Several floors of the building opposite were close enough and high enough to afford a partial vantage of the two men should any cleaner, security guard or some less definable presence be looking down.

Toward the walled edge of the roof were two satellite dishes. One was the same size as a paddling pool, the other three times that. The two of them took cover between the satellite dishes and the wall. If someone was indeed watching them, the view they'd get would be from the shoulders up.

The carrier bag Staunch was carrying and which down on the street had been inaudible began to emit wild crinkling sounds. These were amplified by the hushed roof. Brisk and businesslike, Staunch set down his groceries.

There was no time to express reverence or appreciation so Staunch knelt as if embarking on a chore that had got to be got out of the way quickly. Staunch nipped at the sides of the winter thobe, hoisting it. The youth brought a hand to his chest and held the folds of the garment to his breastbone. Staunch risked pause to savour easing down the undertrousers – a garment which came down to the knees – enough to reveal an inch or so of the underwear beneath, also brilliant white. Of the same almost-gossamer material as the outer britches, the underwear was shorter; the geometry of its cargo straining in abject invitation. Staunch hooked a couple of fingers over both waistbands at once – and tugged.

Staunch sips hot lemon in the sepulchral kitchen while the storm rattles the window frames. This ghostly percussion ushers back the recollection of meeting, three or four contracts ago, a lovelorn mud engineer called Randy at an expatriate party in Abu Dhabi – who confided that he had been thrown over by a cousin who had started going out with girls. It broke his heart, some slut getting that thing. Not 'him' but his 'thing.' Disconcerted, Staunch tried to reason, 'But what about…?' 'meaningful relationship,' 'mutual respect' and 'unconditional…' something or other. (He had had all the jargon to hand in those days.)

'No,' Randy sighed, 'I just want to get my hands on that whopper. On a regular basis.'

Staunch had laughed. It seemed so outrageous. But the mud engineer had been perfectly serious. Now, after all this time, Staunch can see that Randy's had been the sincere remark. That's what had occasioned such amusement; a truth not often unwrapped. The mud engineer had been free of the demands of the unseen-but-always-heard spectre which dictated terms – impossibly reasonable terms – to Staunch. Set against the line Staunch found himself vouchsafing (adopted for fear of – what? Of being castigated by the inner voice of a ruthlessly balanced social hygienist?), the other man's view was less confused, less spurious.

Staunch went on to point out that Randy used the vocabulary of the pornographic magazine when he referred to his beloved. It was all anatomical.

'Why not?' Randy exclaimed, 'Surely you don't want medical terms?'

'It sounds frivolous.'

'When I use those words, frivolous is the last thing I'm being. Far from it. Phrases like "pocket-rocket," "drool-tool" and "tonsil-tickler" save wear and tear on the important words. That way, they're prevented from becoming shop-soiled. Also, porn terminology acts like silver foil. It keeps my preoccupation fresh.'

Musing over his part in these exchanges is, to Staunch, like coming across a shirt he can't believe he ever wore.

What was revealed by the tug set off an inchoate fretting in Staunch. Sight was followed in delirious succession by touch and taste.

One hand by his side, the other holding up his shirt, the figure in black stood; all masculine obedience. This docility was very erotic following the initial pushiness. Beside them, satellite dishes had been cocked to catch God knew what round-the-clock rubbish.

From the start of his ministrations Staunch feared something parting him from his catch. So, with his free hand, he searched his pockets for a scrap of paper. Finding that the only paper he had on him was the wrapping around a tube of mints, he unwound the paper, tore it off and asked the youth for a pen. Shirt hoisted and underwear round his ankles, the Arab patted himself about the chest and found one. Staunch stood up and wrote his telephone number – the ink in the pen was red – and asked the man to write his. The youth recited a few numbers in whispered, hesitant English. When Staunch read the numbers back to him, he faltered at the phrase 'double three.' Staunch showed him what he'd written and asked if it was right. The young Arab listened intently.

'Yes,' he replied.

It wasn't so much the Arab – in all his averageness – Staunch wanted to befriend as the part of him that was least average. That was what Staunch wanted to get to know. However, a rooftop in a black-windowed canyon was not the place to make its acquaintance.

'*Bokura*,' Staunch suggested. 'Tomorrow. Eight o'clock.'

'Fuck, fuck,' the man urged, his entire body struggling with the task of pulling Staunch round. Not threateningly – imploringly. As persistent as a little boy, this big boy must have his way – now. Nothing else existed.

In the tussle he tried to pull down Staunch's jeans without unfastening either belt or buttons. Staunch almost laughed at this desperate scramble. But the youth was serious.

'Fuck, fuck.' It was plea, protest and pitch. His face was etched with the miser's terror of being cheated.

They moved over – part remonstrance, part dance – so that the youth's back was almost against the wall. During this skirmish the black braided cord that fitted over his head-dress fell to the ground. The youth snatched it up off the floor as if the floor was a disgrace, an insult. He fitted it back on his head as though ceremonially correcting a wrong. Then in an urgency of gathered-up garments he leaned forward and began sucking – almost biting – Staunch's bottom lip. Staunch reached for the Arab's balls and started to coddle them; partly for the pleasure of doing so, partly as insurance against ever more painful toothwork.

They were on the roof for nearly half an hour.

'I'll phone you at eight, okay?' Staunch said as he made his way to the door.

Busy with a tissue, the youth offered a muted but still urgent 'My friend...'

Earlier that evening, before setting out on his errand, Staunch took from a glass shelf in the cabinet the wrapper torn from the tube of mints. He picked the scrap up as if any handling other than reverential would damage it.

An abrupt sense of alarm made him compare the number on last night's scrap to a few of the other mobile numbers he'd not yet flung out. He took his address book from the drawer. The number he'd been given on the rooftop was a digit less than that of the others. He rang the number. What he heard was not the ringing tone, nor a dead line. Just a droning sound. He put down the receiver and went upstairs to get ready.

Amid the hiss and steam of the shower, the present tense insinuated itself, whispering; *but he still has your number, hasn't he?* His body warm and lathered; jets of water hitting his back full force, Staunch ignored this. Musings of this sort had been painful at the age of twenty-one but now (soaping his armpits) he no longer possessed the capacity to taunt himself as energetically as he once did. Re-inflictions are for those who didn't take enough notice on previous staggers down the Via Dolorosa.

The present tense – full of its usual gall – repeated its query.

'Ah,' Staunch sang into the spray, as if his reply were part of an aria, 'a couple of decades too late to clutch at such straws, I fear...'

Imagine not being able to recite your own telephone number!

His irritation didn't last long. By the time Staunch ran a towel back and forth across his shoulders, he was sure that if the rooftop lad had set out to give a false number he'd have given the correct amount of digits. The fact that he'd been struggling in a language not his own to recite his telephone number (with shirt up and underwear down) was proof of the authenticity of the young Arab's efforts. It must be. What made it worse – or better: Staunch was convinced that the number was wrong due to incompetence or nerves, not deceit. What had a few minutes ago seemed like stupidity quickly transmogrified into a mystique that deepened the attraction. And compounded the delectable frustration.

Preparing to leave, Staunch was smarting from and sulking over the Dolorosa of knowing what will probably happen but going along anyway. And the humiliation of having common sense kidnapped and held to ransom by the irrefutable seduction of *this* time.

The city was comparatively deserted. There were few people about. Too few. Staunch felt conspicuous. Along the stretch of catwalk he looked neither left nor right. A police car dozed in wait outside the shopping centre. Another Station of the Cross: heading back to the Same Place at the Same Time armed with nothing but a feeling indistinguishable from desperation. But which Staunch supposed was hope.

His *raison d'être* for the evening wrapped in plastic and hanging on hooks from his thumb, Staunch began to think he'd completed his mission too soon. Swanning around with dry cleaning over his shoulder for over an hour hadn't been part of his plan. However, his haste to get into town and demonstrate a purpose (other than the real one) had made it so. Convinced that he'd see the youth again – how could the figure in the long black shirt not be at the parking bays at the same time tonight as he was last night? – Staunch could even envisage the casual look of surprise which would cross his face as he saw the lad again.

While he waited for the hour to approach Staunch decided to pass the time in Moorish café across the street from the party supplies shop. Once seated, he felt calm among the men. His thoughts flailed less. The most sullen of the waiters appeared and took his order of Turkish coffee and a thyme croissant.

Zhata. That's Arabic for thyme. The herb is crushed very fine, almost to a powder, before it is folded into the pastry. Slowly tearing the croissant had the effect of making him reflective.

Years ago in a San Francisco coffee shop he saw pinned to a corkboard a notice of a forthcoming public lecture. It stated venue, starting time, the speaker's name and the opportunity for questions afterwards. The title of the talk was 'Are You a Size Queen?' Staunch wondered where the possibility existed for any form of doubt, elaboration or discussion. Who would fuss at, worry over and intellectualize a question that could yield only a simple yes or no? Now he wished he had attended. Amid all the jargon, cerebration and exegesis someone might have solved the mystery of why being enamoured in this way is no less worthy than being captivated by an expressive chipped tooth or the ineffable pattern of dark hair on a stranger's forearms.

Men were coming in from the terrace. The beginnings of a sandstorm were swirling rags of paper, flinging cardboard containers blotched by the grease of onion rings: lifting them higher than the surrounding buildings. Some customers wrapped the lower part of their head-dress round their mouths. Others turned their faces away.

No one in his right mind would be hanging around outside on a night like this.

Staunch wiped as much of the green powder as he could from his fingers. Earlier he had been too distraught over the missing digit to entertain the suspicion that, after several bouts, he'd get used to the object of his anthropomorphism. Take it for granted. After not very long perhaps he'd see only the petulant little boy.

There were no cars let alone people outside the party supplies shop.

The real Calvary: *He had known.* Something deeper than hope had known all along that when prowling around in the present tense there is no need for the past – or the future.

Staunch squeezed himself and his dry cleaning through a sparse patch of the hedge in the dividing strip between the café side of the road and the side with the parking bays. He'd just got through the scrub and was waiting to cross when his eyes, ears and mouth were hit by the wind – and the sand carried in it. Hearing rather than seeing that there were no cars coming, he ran across the road. Shielding his eyes with one hand, holding the wire coat hangers with the other, Staunch hailed a taxi with his foot.

He gave the name of his compound.

'One dinar-fifty.'

'Okay.'

He laid the shirts on the back seat and sat in front. His palms were mauve and white, stinging from the wire hooks.

'Going home?'

'Yes.'

Every time the taxi stopped at a red light, the driver groped himself. Under normal circumstances Staunch would have been tempted. Now, though, he was apprehensive: if he went ahead and responded to the offer but if what he had a feel of wasn't in the same league as the last one, the tactile memory of the night before would be partly expunged. So he pretended not to recognize the invitation.

Tapping the packet of sugar with a cardboard bow tie; from bottom to top, carefully, as if expecting the next tap to yield something surprising, Staunch sees the sugar as a connection with the person – the penis – on the rooftop.

Out of *that* present a memento for *this* moment.

The storm is still raging.

He must go to bed now. Removing the assortment of objects from the kitchen table, Staunch drops the laundry bow ties into the pedal bin then switches off the kitchen counter lights. Making his way upstairs he tells himself he'll not be beaten – not even by that most persistent of Dolorosas; the hope that one present tense soon, the past might inadvertently repeat itself.

Recovery

– Charles Wilkinson –

The deterioration in my eyesight has been most welcome. I need only take off my glasses to defamiliarize the world: the scene outside the bus now fur-like, the fuzz on the peach of the day – and on the hoardings great yellow suns that could be oranges. Only the largest street signs are legible. Shops fronts have names but offer blurred services. The scaffolding on the red-brick building that I know to be a library looks softer, frayed at the edges like rope. Women, smudged black *niqabs*, make their way to the supermarket; their grey-paint shadows run off them. Faces have lost their hard lines. Even the man three seats in front of me has a comfortable haze of white hair. I prefer it this way. I am sitting right at the back of the bus, protecting myself with Victor Shklovsky. I am not just a man, wearing a crumpled linen jacket and trousers that have no creases, on a bus heading into the centre of Birmingham: I have heard of Viktor Shklovsky; even read Victor Shklovsky – though a long time ago. I had tenure.

An advantage of my condition is that I can now read without my glasses. If here, this minute, this second, I wish to embrace the pleasures of the text, I have only to glance down at my bus ticket. It is, admittedly, no substitute for the works of the great Russian formalist, but to a cultural critic everything is interesting. In a few minutes the bus will reach Highgate, so very unlike its London eponym: wasteland, weeds, gardens of tarmac; low level flats' concrete dentistry; the Gothic church that served the poor; nineteenth-century warehouses awaiting boho restoration, one a community centre, others roofless, half mortared with birds' nests and wild grass. And then the human traces, found on the net: a sniper firing at random from a tower block; a man discovered in Gooch Street burning like a torch; a resident convicted of unlawful storage of fireworks. Permission has been granted for a sheep pen at the Pak Mecca Meals Abattoir.

Keidrych Gomer-Price, a man who embodied a tradition in himself, the first and last of the great Welsh-Birmingham modernist poets, lived here – the only permanent resident in what is now the Paragon Hotel. These are the streets through which he walked composing uniquely radical verse, subversive and formally inventive in its intentions: what was to become the most unjustly ignored body of work in the history of Anglo-Welsh twentieth-century poetry. Was he my brother's lover? Inspector Davenport didn't think so.

Towards the end of my teaching career at a small private university on the west coast of America, I surprised my colleagues by ceasing to publish in the field of cultural theory and returning to what I suppose could be called my early enthusiasms. As a young associate professor, I had published papers on Pound, Zukofsky and the Objectivists; a monograph on Olson's poetics and his use of projective verse in Maximus appeared from a small academic press. This is what I did not tell them: it was discovery of some of Gomer-Price's manuscripts – including the manuscript of a long poem that scholars believed had disappeared when he moved from his mother's house at Balsall Heath to his flat in the Paragon Hotel – that had attracted my attention. There was also, of course, the matter of my brother's murder.

I did not hurry to cross the Atlantic. There were many letters to be written and a great deal of the preliminary research could be done at the university. When a literary discovery is also material evidence in a murder case, there is always the possibility of the scene becoming overcrowded with expert witnesses. I decided to wait. Only three people have published on Gomer-Price in the last twenty years: one, at the University of Notre Dame in Indiana, suffers from uncertain health; the second, a young lady from the University of Helsinki, is on sabbatical leave in Peru. Only Tod Hitzlesperger, from one of the Cambridge colleges, would have been at all likely to act before me, and I knew that his book on Prynne was overdue. And as for Inspector Davenport, I very much doubted that he was a subscriber to the *Journal of Experimental and Innovative Verse*.

Canting to the left allows the bus to tuck in near the ancient market site. Only the Rotunda recognisable on its ridge. Passengers alight for the Bullring Centre. St Martin's brick is a brighter red. Sequinned Selfridge's has discs that dress up light. Yet the sense of previous space haunts: the subterranean market stalls, the long yacht-white building above, the mural of the black bull in relief on its side, always smaller than expected. And behind this, another market visited in my childhood, something so delicate it can now hardly be visualised. Nothing more than the texture of a time when I was smaller and geometry different. How many Bull Rings live here?

As I walk up towards New Street, I can hear the sentences in my head regaining grammatical formality. Every step punctuates. Surprise and nostalgia, I tell myself, disintegrate syntax. It will be important to think clearly. Leaving for America was a way of living in every moment. Under new skies it is less easy to be ambushed by the past. When I arrived they had only just started to the build the university. There were no courtyards with statues or fountains, no oil paintings of past Deans to hang on the walls, no distinguished alumni, names and traditions to be remembered or lived up to. I watched glass and steel rise impersonally on land that had known nothing heavier than the tread of bison. This dream of academia always looked set to vanish in an instant, ready to accept the return of grass.

The cry of gulls. I do not remember that sound here. Birmingham becoming Brighton beach. For a second I feel as if I am on the coast, the sharp salt in the air, the shingle under my feet. Then it's gone and I am wondering what happened to the great flocks of starlings, settling, wheeling into the damp grey day, only to fall farther away, diminished to specks of soot. By the statue of Queen Victoria I compose myself when I recall my life. I have a number of papers in my bag and none of them relate to ornithology. I am anxious to limit my time in this city and must not allow myself to be distracted.

I have already been here for a week, and must confess that I have achieved a great deal less than I would have liked. Tomorrow's meeting with Luke Hale at the Paragon Hotel will determine whether my visit has been a success. As I walk up the steps to the Central Library, the ghost of a building in Ratcliffe Place rises up, the sweep of its marble staircase leading to a high vaulted ceiling, colonnades, walls lined with books, old leather and paper smell, tickets to be filled in, the long wait for a return from the stacks. My happiest days were here.

Of course you knew that though I used the present tense it was all in the past, fading before I even wrote it. And afterwards every phrase fixed it differently on the sheet that is never white but always stained, however faintly, with what went before. I have learnt to distrust the artifice of story. Even the narrative of a simple bus journey is not innocent enough.

It is ten years since I was in this city. I came to bury my brother, and so it was hard to explain why I arrived before his death. Inspector Davenport, I remember, disliked my assertion that I always had an instinct for what was about happen. I stuck to simple statements of fact. If he wished to construct a case, impose his storyline on discrete material, spend some time manipulating the few shreds of available evidence, then that was entirely up to him. I would answer questions, in the presence of my solicitor, but I would not be a narrator, reliable or otherwise. It was shortly after this, when they decided to drop the case and I was free to return to America, that I began to appreciate reflexive, non-linear poetry. Now that I was no longer teaching in the English Department I was free to read for myself in the evenings. There was no longer that constriction of always being on the look-out for work that would appeal to my students. These new texts resisted hermeneutic closure and, knowing that I would not be called upon to interpret them, I was free to respond to a dizzying new lexis of freedom: the flux and fold of language, the words barely anchored to the page, meanings that flickered then withdrew, and each reading a fresh reception, the exhilaration of the constantly replenished text. All of this, I discovered, was at its best after three large glasses of white wine.

For some time I'd known that my brother had been a friend of Keidrych Gomer-Price, though I'd never read that poet's work. It was whilst I was on vacation after the Fall Semester that I discovered a rare edition of his Selected Poems published by the Sparrowhawk Press in 1958. On my previous visit to Birmingham, I had become aware of rumours that my brother's young flesh had consoled the poet in his final years, but I determined to read these verses in the disinterested spirit of true criticism. I retreated to my hotel with one of the finest Sauvignons that California has to offer and by the time that I had finished the bottle I was convinced that I was in the presence of great poetry. For a month or two, I gave serious consideration to writing a brief article on Gomer-Price for a small journal in Lampeter, but in the end I decided against this. It was only after I heard of Luke Hale's discovery that my interest was reignited.

I dressed carefully for my visit to Highgate. Although I have always known how to appear on important occasions, I felt that this was not the time to wear my Tom Wolfe white suit. Playing the southern gentleman on the streets of inner-city Birmingham would only attract attention. I wore a blue jacket with a collar and tie and concealed even this low level formality beneath a baggy fleece. I polished but did not shine my shoes.

These preparations came to seem unnecessary when I got off the bus at Bradford Street and found the place deserted, apart from an elderly Chinese woman waiting at the stop on the other side of the road. A few threads of sunlight fell from the battlements of unmoving castles of clouds. I turned left and there, a little way along, was the Paragon Hotel: vast Victorian Gothic, its brick almost mellow, pale orange mixed with the lightest of browns, and yet the whole of it erected on too huge a scale to be homely: turrets at the four corners topped with lilac hats; a few wide windows on the ground floor, then smaller at each level, suggesting a multiplicity of tiny rooms – those near the top being perhaps no more than cubicles. For what purpose it had been built was not immediately apparent to me.

Inside was spacious, comfortably furnished and filled with priests and nuns. As I made my way towards the bar, I saw that one of the rooms had been converted into a temporary chapel. A home-made sign gave the times for Mass. An elderly man in a black suit walked towards me, his red and slightly puffy features raw from the winds on an Irish farm. A long table had been placed in the corridor and the woman behind it, who had been arranging pamphlets, glanced up, and gave me part of a smile as she assessed me for religious affiliations.

Three priests stood at the bar drinking Guinness. There was only one table where every seat had not been taken. A man with black hair and regular features sat alone with a shiny leather briefcase unopened in front of him. His skin had an unnatural smoothness but was so pale that I thought his veins must lie weirdly deep.

'Luke Hale?' I asked.

He nodded. Although he appeared so much younger than I had expected, his eyes had the surface glint of coal, a suggestion of something that had long been buried underground and now recovered for the fall of light.

'I read your article in the *Journal of Experimental and Innovative Poetry*. It was most interesting, I thought.'

'Thank you.' His voice was neutral.

He was wearing a well-cut business suit with an expensive sheen. He had nothing of the academic about him. I tried to imagine him on campus, talking to students, lecturing, drinking bitter coffee in the senior common room. Which university was he at? Then I remembered that his biographical note had been uninformative: simply a list of some previous publications on writers of whom I had not heard.

'I'm sorry,' I said, 'I've forgotten where you teach.'

'I am not attached,' he replied evenly, 'to any particular institution.'

'How did you come to be working on Keidrych Gomer-Price?'

For a second it occurred to me that this man might have been one of the poet's lovers, although he had about him a hint of something crueller than sex, a dark refinement dredged up from a Renaissance court. Then I realised that he could have been no more than a very small boy at the time of the poet's death.

'I think, Dr Hopton, that you are hear to learn more about my discoveries. So much of what I found out did not, as I am sure you have been able to guess, appear in the article. But then, of course, it was of only biographical importance. And since the death of the author there has been so much more interest in texts.'

A sound like the snap of fingers on thumbs as the briefcase sprang open, its quivering lid concealing the contents from view. Hales took out what I soon saw was a large manila envelope, which he handed to me.

'None of this will come as a great surprise to you. I have kept the originals.'

'I will be returning to America towards the end of next week, but we could meet…'

'I know all about you,' he said. 'One does not have to be at a university to do research.'

He shut the briefcase and rose to his feet. As he walked away from me, the door opened and then, after a sea of thirsty priests – blushing country-faces, silver-hair, huge parishioner-greeting hands – flooded in, I heard it swing to. Hales, moving with surprising celerity for one so pale, was soon among them; in seconds both the briefcase and he had disappeared from view. I stood up so that I could see over the gleaming crests of clerical heads. The door did not open. Soon the priests were dispersing to tables and the bar – and there was no one there.

I have put the previous section in the past tense because that is where I would have liked to have kept it. Now the events which I described have formed themselves into lines, threatening all that is to come with closure. For a long time, I sat at the table, the manila envelope still sealed on the table in front me. Each time the door opened I looked up, but Hales did not re-enter the room. I was still not sure that he had ever left it. After I had bought myself another drink I returned circuitously, so as to inspect the faces at each table and see if Hales had insinuated himself among them to observe me from a distance. There was no sign of him.

The conversation of the priests became louder, their laughter took on a sharper edge, their eyes seemed smaller, glinting with foul merriment; and, as the evening wore itself away, their clerical garments moved one shade closer to night: as if Hale had vanished by transforming himself into a thousand pieces so that he might more easily hide his darkness in them. I told myself that I must continue to think clearly, grammatically. I had been stupid to think that by meeting with Hales I could force a compromise. Convince him that it was impossible for me to accede to his demands. Afterwards I believed that by giving me the documents, revealing all that he had against me, he meant to suggest he would return, and we would talk again. This was a delusion that was destined to last for less than two minutes more: the length of time it took me to pick up the envelope, get up, leave the bar and make my way into the lobby where the doors of the lift opened with a derisive lisp and Inspector Davenport stepped out in front of me.

'The dog returns to its vomit, I see. Welcome back to Birmingham, Dr. Hopton.' He stretched out his right hand and I gave him the manila envelope.

Now I am seated at the window of my ground floor room in the small hotel where I have been staying these past few weeks. My passport is in the possession of Inspector Davenport and I have been told that I am not to leave the city. A bright day in the last week of March is fading slowly to dusk; a glossy blue sky, yellowish white light behind the gables of pink brick houses The trees are still bare, though as I type, I can hear the tune of an ice cream van heralding summer. I shall be grateful if it stays fine for my last days of freedom. I have tried so hard not to make this into a story. But the mistakes that I made have allowed them to construct a narrative around me. At least, I shall try not to end with a dying fall.

There are day, months and even a year when we have no idea what happened in the life of Keidrych Gomer-Price. In the last decade, a few surviving friends from school and university have been tracked down and interviewed, but their memories are vague, partial, contradictory, incomplete, offering no more than a wraith of the poet in his youth. Some documentation and manuscripts have been found. Yet what is recovered is always so much less than what is lost. This is what I have come to accept.

I have been here for some time. The tree across the street is dying. In the weakening light, its branches seem broken: strokes of Japanese calligraphy on a background of dark blue linen. A wall hanging washed by a thousand evenings, its meaning fading into the fabric. I said that this is how I would not finish. They have their own narratology: those manuals of procedures, codes of practice that define each element of the story. They will move me through their opening paragraphs: standard caution, interview and arrest; the triple climax of indictment, committal, trial will lead to the sentence with the final twist.

Now that they have arrived I can see that their uniforms match the sky. Only Inspector Davenport stands out, his long mackintosh the colour of the stone-white moon. They have opened the gate, but I will wait for them to walk up to the door. There will be more words and a warrant. Now the bell ringing, the hammering of the brass knocker – I will heed the head of a lion.

I darken the screen and press delete. As the text vanishes, they stop knocking. Perhaps they sense that I am about to come to the door. My hands close the laptop, as if pressing down on a coffin's lid. It is always so hard to know what will remain, even when so little has been saved.

Siramina

– M. Pinchuk –

I had arrived from the mainland on the afternoon ferry, the only tourist on board. It had been blazingly sunny when we left – in fact, it had been sunny for the whole month I'd been in the country – but about halfway through the crossing, the sun disappeared and the rain bucketed down. The locals seemed to expect the wet weather: they all carried umbrellas or rain ponchos. I'd had to dash for cover and then root around in my suitcase for ages before I found my raincoat. Most passengers stayed on deck, facing down the storm with loud talk, and drinking home-brewed alcohol from jam-jars. I wasn't brave enough to join them. I spent the journey inside, huddled near the door, trying to keep my mind off the stench of mould and sweat, wondering where the sudden rain had come from. I caught sight of the world outside only when the door opened to let people in or out.

The rain washed away all colour, painting the sea and sky an even, pearly grey. In the depths of the downpour the horizon disappeared, and I lost my sense of direction.

When we docked, the crowd from the ferry dispersed quickly into waiting cars, the arms of family, the sodden air. I sheltered under the awning that spanned the entrance to the terminal.

The night clerk at a hotel on the coast had got me into this. It was late in the season, and I'd been one of only a handful of guests. He spent most of his time drinking espressos that he made in the restaurant after it closed, but one night he offered me a whisky, so I took the opportunity to ask for recommendations of places to see. He thought for a moment, smoothing a hand over his dark handlebar moustache. *I've heard Siramina is a special place*, he said, *very unusual.*

I couldn't find it in my guidebook.

Everyone says things are easy there, he encouraged me, If you have time, I think you must go.

He mentioned that only one hotel was open at this time of year. But, of course, there is a tourism office just before the ferry building, and someone will help you. You will have no problems.

I pulled up my hood and walked from under the awning. The rain had melted into a heavy drizzle, muddling the air and fraying the outlines of the small park in front of the terminal.

A temporary-looking building squatted on the edge of the park, off to my left. Bright blue paint peeled from the textured aluminium siding, and mildew stretched into lopsided spider webs in the corners of the windows. I cupped my hands around my face and peered in. There was a stack of paper towels on a desk. A few faded brochures littered the floor. I turned away, hoping to find someone who could point me towards the hotel. But the fog settling over the terminal hid anyone who might have been there.

I decided to trust my luck.

With the station at my back, I headed into Siramina. I'd picked up a map before boarding the ferry and knew that one of Siramina's main streets started on the far side of the park. It was sure to lead to some sort of central area where I could get information or maybe find the hotel itself. As I crossed the intersection, a dog barked twice and another howled in reply, but I couldn't tell where the sound came from.

Wind blew the rain into my face. It hung on the edges of my hood, smearing my ears and forehead with cool water.

According to my map, the street ran north-south through the city. It was lined with clothing shops, bakeries, cafés, all of them closed: shutters were pulled down and some were locked with two padlocks. In the middle of the next block, a podgy man and a slim woman, their clothes glistening greenly, kept their heads down as they drifted across the street holding hands.

I walked on for a few blocks and noticed that the names of the side streets didn't correspond to their names on my map. Maybe streets changed their names in different parts of the city, or maybe the map was out of date. Raindrops splattered the map, smudging boundaries and place names; the paper pulled apart along the creases where it had been folded. I balled up the map and dropped it in a rubbish bin.

I decided that the best course was to continue following the main street. As I got closer to the centre of town, there were sure to be adverts, and maybe even another tourist information office. I pulled my hood tighter around my face. Up ahead, a man in an aqua raincoat shimmering with the iridescence of fish scales, hunched his shoulders against the weather. I hurried to catch up with him. *Please excuse me*, I called, *Good day, excuse me please, please.*

The man stopped and turned to face me, blinking his hazel-coloured eyes rapidly as if he were surprised. His long, pale lashes seemed to end in fine droplets of rain. His arms cradled an oblong box of sweets wrapped in paper from a bakery that was spoken about on the mainland. I asked carefully if he knew the hotel.

He shrugged, lowered his eyes.

I repeated the name.

He shifted the package in his arms; the damp left translucent fingerprints on the paper. He waved his hand, indicating the way I was already headed. I thanked him. He gave me a faded smile and disappeared around the next corner.

I seemed to be on the right path, so I kept going until, after a few minutes, I saw a place where the mist shaped vague halos around a line of dim lights. I headed for them, envisioning a warm and lively restaurant or, at least, a café, someplace where I could ask for directions.

The lights were actually lanterns, strung under tarps arranged to form makeshift roofs for about three or four street stalls. As a concession to the weather, goods were displayed under clear plastic sheets. There was an amazing array of merchandise: roughly knitted sweaters, cheap-looking alarm clocks and watches, camp stoves, CDs, old mirrors that had lost some of their silvering.

I was sure someone there would be able to help.

I asked a guy selling incense and candles whether I might find the hotel along the main street. I pronounced the name carefully. A wide streak of blond disrupted his dark hair. He looked right into my eyes and then he turned away, coughing nervously and busying himself rearranging a pile of cardboard boxes. Something about him made me think he hadn't been on the island for very long. The next stall sold those painted Russian dolls that fit one inside another, necklaces made out of large chunks of amber, random pieces of tarnished cutlery and a couple of ancient pistols inlaid with mother of pearl. The woman behind the stall was reading a paperback written in an alphabet I didn't recognize. With her auburn hair and high cheekbones, she was clearly a foreigner too. I phrased the question in my head and let the words trickle out carefully. *Have you, excuse me, any knowledge of the hotel for which I search?* She replied that she did not know it. I named the hotel again but with a different inflection, trying to remember how the night clerk had pronounced it. The woman sighed, then pointed up the street. I tried to ask how far it was to the hotel, but either she didn't understand me or she didn't know. *Old city, old city,* she said and picked up her book. Before she turned away I noticed that although her eyes were dark, each had an unexpected splash of pale blue.

I thanked her as best I could and started up the street. On I walked, past restaurants that were closed, bars that were closed. Newsagents, doctors' offices, cigarette kiosks, all of them closed. Occasionally I thought I saw people walking towards me, but our paths never crossed.

I stopped at every traffic light even though I hadn't seen any cars. At one corner, I was debating how far to continue along the main street when I happened to glance up. Through a shift in the mist, I saw a small yellow sign. Written in black was the name of the hotel. An arrow pointed to the left. It seemed to be five hundred metres ahead. At last.

The street I turned onto was narrower than the main street, just about wide enough for a small car with a careful driver. There were no sidewalks, so I kept as far to one side as I could, avoiding the puddles growing haphazardly on the paving. I felt confident that at any minute an illuminated yellow sign would appear and then the entrance to the hotel: wood doors with glass panes through which I would see welcoming lights, a thick russet-coloured carpet, and a clerk with a gentle expression standing behind the burnished wood of the reception desk. The rooms would be cheerful, painted in bright colours, and well lit to remind guests it was actually late summer despite the fact that you couldn't see the sky or the sun. The clerk would offer me a hot drink and maybe a tray of home-baked pastries. I wondered if the pastries would be similar to those on the mainland, which were made from a sweet dough stuffed with chopped nuts and fruit.

At a Y-shaped intersection a building loomed out of the grey like a ship. I was certain the hotel was housed inside, if it didn't take up the whole building itself. But though I walked completely around it and tried all the doors, I couldn't find the hotel. I looked back to where I thought the main street should be but thick fog drifted and hovered like a seabird uncertain where to land, obscuring the end of the street.

Instinct told me to take the fork to the left, or maybe it wasn't instinct: it was my dependence on that one sign. So I headed into the spiralling mist and felt it wrap around me like an overcoat of clouds.

Buildings towered over me, making this street feel even more confining than the last. On my left, there was an unbroken line of shops on the ground floor, flats above, and laundry that had been hung out to dry but instead released its own heavy drops. I glimpsed someone behind a window and smiled. I started to speak, then realised I was looking at myself: my hair plastered to my face by the rain looked darker than usual, as did my eyes. I nodded to myself in the window and continued on.

To my right, there was a rough wall, the top of which had crumbled away, exposing cracks running like rivers. But as I looked up, my eyes found a bit of yellow with black lettering and an arrow pointing in the direction I was going.

It couldn't be too much further.

I ploughed on for another ten minutes or so, shifting my suitcase from my left hand to my right and back again. I was sure to end up with blisters. Eventually, the street widened into a small plaza with a dribbling fountain at its centre. The water in the fountain was covered with a thin blanket of green scum, its surface pocked by the fat raindrops now falling. The remains of a market were scattered across the cobbled square: piles of rotting vegetables, discarded plastic bags, cigarette butts, and bones still bloody from recent butchering. A few straw-coloured cats perched on a battered garbage can, hissing at one another and eyeing the scraps heaped inside. The square was the most open place I'd been for a while, but even it was overhung with a translucent scrim of coalescing fog.

I stood near the fountain and turned around and around, looking for the hotel or anything that would lead me to it. The buildings surrounding the plaza had been impressive once, with their tall, narrow windows and elegant shutters. And I was sure they had been painted bright, warm colours: terracottas and pinks and ochres.

But the colour had washed out of the paint long ago, and many of the balconies were gone. Those that remained had chunks of plaster missing from their undersides, and ironwork mottled with rust that looked like a fungus.

Voices, raised and angry, stitched their way through the soggy air. I wheeled around, and came face to face with a tightly shuttered building. The incessant rain was playing tricks with sound. But maybe the hotel was nearby and I'd just heard the tail-end of a row in the kitchen: some temperamental chef berating his assistant for undercooking the carrots or leaving the meringues in the oven too long.

I decided to walk for five or ten minutes down each of the streets leading off the square. I was sure I would find the hotel. I turned once more and when I chose a street, it was almost as if my feet knew where to take me.

The street became an alley where it left the square. It was chock-a-block with buildings of different shapes and sizes, all in various stages of disrepair. I thought I heard thunder, still far-off, but maybe it was only the sound of the sea. There was a sign up ahead, though it didn't look yellow.

Perhaps it was the hotel after all or, maybe, a cigarette kiosk.

My suitcase bumped against the stucco walls of the houses, rattling the painted metal doors. I walked towards the sign and found a small sandwich shop. I realized I hadn't eaten since before leaving the mainland. Through the window I saw an old man and woman clearing tables and putting containers into a refrigerator. When I walked in, the woman looked up from wrapping a large piece of cheese. Her eyes were a liquid blue and her fair, almost colourless, hair was pulled back from her plump face. She said something too quickly for me to understand. I smiled and pushed my way between the chairs and tables that crowded the floor. *Good day*, I said enunciating carefully.

She realised I hadn't understood her and spoke louder. *Welcome early evening*, she corrected, *after this time the shops on Sunday are not open.*

I nodded. *Please, I understand*, I told her, and then I asked for the hotel. She frowned and shook her head, went back to stretching cling film across bowls. The old man came over, looked at me as if I were a puzzle he had no solution for. *Where?* he asked. He was round and balding with eyes slightly lighter blue than the woman's. A white T-shirt stretched lazily across his stomach like a comfortable yawn.

I tried to pronounce the name of the hotel correctly. He exchanged a few words with the old woman. *Yes, yes*, he said, *up this street my friend, my guest. You will find it.*

I thank you, I said, would it be impossible to have a small sandwich, outside to be eaten?

I am sorry, he said, for now it is not possible.

He patted my back and guided me to the door, talking a-mile-a-minute. He shook my hand. I stepped over the threshold, and he pointed further along the alley. *The hotel for which you search in that direction is,* he said slowly, then closed the door and locked it. He smiled as he pulled down the shade.

I marched on with renewed confidence.

But although I walked for what I guessed was fifteen minutes, I came across no other people and no hotel. So I stopped. I stood in the middle of the alley. The houses on either side rose so high they seemed to lean slightly inward, as if they might meet somewhere far above my head. Rain and a distinct rolling of thunder filled the air. A short way along, there was a break in the line of houses on my right and there was a wall. And behind the farthest end of the wall was an elongated dome with a cross.

Of course: it was Sunday. Everyone was in church. Surely, someone there would help me find the hotel.

The entrance to the churchyard was down a passage so narrow I had to scuttle through at an angle like a land crab on damp sand. A door in the wall was open and led into a garden. Two rows of small trees flanked a gravel path strewn with puddles. The trees were bent low by the water weeping from their leaves; the patchy grass under them was pale and unkempt. The path led to a plaza. A few benches were arranged awkwardly in the centre. I could almost see the paint starting to peel off them and splinters working themselves loose from the rain-swollen wood.

I brushed my dripping hair from my eyes and studied the church looming over the plaza. Then I climbed twelve rain-slickened stone steps up to it, my suitcase bumping against each one. I slipped on the last step and skidded towards the rough, stone wall. I reached out to steady myself and managed to keep from falling, but my hand came away from the wall covered in brownish slime. I had nothing to wipe it off with, so I held my palm up to the sky and watched rain collect on it. Then I turned my palm down and watched the water and slime run off.

I pushed the dark-wood door, but it wouldn't budge. The church had to be open. I leaned my shoulder against the door, heard a creak, and pushed harder. It opened suddenly and I stumbled inside.

I set my suitcase down, stood with my back against the door until I got my bearings and my eyes adjusted to the dimness. There was no congregation and no priest: just me, some erratically placed electric lights and a few sputtering candles. I walked through the vestibule and down the nave, trailing my fingers along the tops of the pews. Shards of beige varnish flaked off and stuck to my damp and wrinkled fingers. The altar and the spaces beyond it were dark. Nervously, I sidled into a pew and sat, squinting into the murky air and listening to the quiet contained by the thick-walled building. Then I heard a soft, regular sound, even and steady like a metronome.

My jacket, where it wasn't dripping onto me, was dripping onto the floor. I draped it over the end of the pew. Soon I was again submerged in the hush of the church. And then the ticking of the metronome gently surfaced. The sound came from somewhere off to my right. I walked along the pew to the far aisle, where a handful of candles guttered in front of the statue of a saint I didn't recognise. I worked a candle loose from the wax-encrusted holder and headed for the sound, stepping over a threshold of shadows that was only slightly disturbed by the feeble light in my hand.

I was in a small room. High in the wall, a narrow window let some of the darkness seep out into the woolly-grey mist. I stepped closer to the sound. With my left hand, I found the edge of what I took to be an altar. It was rough, damp stone not smooth, cool marble. I floated my hand over the surface. Water splashed onto the back of my hand once and then again. The noise stopped. I felt a small, mossy depression near the centre of the stone. I pulled my hand away and the sound resumed.

Maybe no one knew about the leak. Maybe I could find someone and tell them about it, and they would help me find the hotel. But though I navigated my way along all the walls of the church and tried every door, I found no one.

I made my way to the entrance. It took several attempts to open the door. Outside, the air had deepened, turned the colour of ripe plums. I tried to see if there was anyone I could tell about the leak, anyone at all. But shadows merged into the darkening evening and no one moved through them. Rain pulsed against the stairs.

I went inside and replaced my candle at the saint's feet. I sat down near my suitcase, and then and there I decided to spend the night in the church. There was nothing else to do really. The churches in Siramina had been known for welcoming travellers since the Middle Ages, and I'd get up early so I wouldn't trouble anyone. Everything would sort itself out in the morning.

There wasn't enough light to read by, so I made a pillow out of my sweater, and a blanket out of an extra shirt and pair of trousers. The pew wasn't the most comfortable bed but I fell asleep almost immediately and dreamed of shadows spreading across the floor, forming bottomless lakes around me.

I slept until a susurrus of murmuring washed over me, pulling me up from the slow-moving depths of sleep. I propped myself on my elbow and looked over the top of the pew. An old woman hunched in front of the altar with her back to me. I sat up quietly and then realized that the lights above the altar were on, picking out a well-weathered crucifix, a cloth embroidered in blues and greens, and a listless bouquet of pallid flowers. I didn't want to interrupt the old woman's prayers, so I waited. The lights over the altar went out. Startled, I stood up. The woman kept murmuring. I heard a clink, and the lights came on again. Still praying, she turned away from a small metal box and faced the altar. I should have known: the lights in the smaller churches on the mainland were coin-operated when services weren't being held.

The old woman finished her prayers before the lights went out a second time and turned to me. *Welcome evening,* she called, her thin voice bouncing off the interior of the dome and rippling towards me. She wore a navy blue apron studded with paler pockets. Her rainboots were pulled over turquoise socks. I ran my fingers through my hair and walked sheepishly down the nave. I didn't know what time it was, but no light came through the windows.

Welcome evening, she said again, shaking my hand.

I tried to imitate her inflection but managed only to garble the words badly.

She held my hand tightly in her cool fingers and looked me over. Her grey eyes glanced at my shoeless feet, my face, and then focused somewhere near my right shoulder. A cloud of silver-white hair bobbed and shimmered around her face. Her smile was more like a half-smile, but it felt friendly. She didn't seem surprised to see me.

She motioned for me to stay where I was, then walked along the side aisle and into the shadows. A deep humming and a thud signalled the turning on of a few more lights. She reappeared and began a tour of the church, studying the floor and occasionally holding her hand out, palm up. I followed. I had no idea what she was searching for. At our third stop, midway along one of the aisles, we found it: a puddle and a steady drip of water. From there she led me, without stopping, to another puddle and then another. I took her to the side chapel; she seemed pleased I had found that leak.

In a far, dark corner of the church, green plastic buckets leaned in a crooked stack slightly taller than the old woman. I placed a bucket under each leak, surprised that there was exactly the right number of them. The old woman smiled and patted me on the back. I followed her to the vestibule, where a brand-new mop was propped in its own bucket. While I mopped the puddles, the old woman checked on the buckets. The rain seemed to be coming down harder, and some of the buckets were halfway full by the time I'd finished. The old woman surveyed my work and the placement of the buckets, and nodded. She retrieved a pinkly pale raincoat from a pew at the back and snugged herself into it. Before leaving, she pointed out the buckets that would soon need emptying.

I walked her to the door and she waved from the bottom of the stairs. I hoped she didn't have far to go: the wind had picked up and drove slanted sheets of rain across the plaza.

I emptied buckets and mopped up spills for most of the night, accompanied by the steady tattoo of drips that acted as a barometer of the storm. Near morning, the rain eased off. A thin light filtered through the windows as I put the mop and its bucket at the end of a pew, and stretched out, wrapped in my extra clothing. I'd just slipped into sleep when I heard, *Welcome morning!* The old woman stood at the end of the pew carrying a grease-stained paper bag. *Welcome morning*, she repeated as I rubbed my eyes and sat up. She went into the shadows, and there was some clattering and the sound of water splashing, and hissing as if from a camp stove. She returned bearing an aluminium tray with two mismatched mugs and the paper bag. I pushed my clothes to one end of the pew and she sat down, placing the tray between us. I waited. She picked up a mug and held it out to me with slightly shaking hands. I could see blue-green veins through her translucent skin.

I took the mug and mumbled a thank you, knowing I'd get the pronunciation wrong. She shrugged. The coffee was instant: bitter and hot. She opened the bag and put two diamond-shaped pastries on the tray, one in front of each of us. They were crumbly and tasted of flowers and herbs, with an interesting salty aftertaste. They were surprisingly filling. While we ate, she gabbled on. I tried to indicate that she was speaking too quickly by shrugging, shaking my head. I picked out a few words – I may have heard the word for foreigner – but after a time, I just smiled and nodded. She seemed to feel that I understood enough of what she said, and she patted me on the knee reassuringly. As soon as we finished our coffee and the crumbs from the pastries, she stood, picked up a large ring of keys from the pew behind us and pointed to my suitcase. I felt silly, embarrassed by the mess of my clothes. She said something. I shook my head. She pushed past, picked up my sweater and folded it. I opened my suitcase, shoved my clothes inside and snapped it shut, giving the combination lock an extra spin. With my suitcase secured and my shoes on (even though they weren't quite dry), I followed her to a small closet at the back of the church. I wasn't certain whether I'd found that door the night before. She tried a few keys before she was able to unlock it and wrestle my suitcase inside. Some blankets were folded neatly on a chair. She pointed at them, pointed at me, and acted out snuggling down underneath them and pulling them up to her chin.

I nodded and smiled, enunciating each syllable as I repeated, *I thank you, I thank you.*

She locked the closet, took a small, hollow key off the ring, placed it in my palm and folded my fingers around it. We walked to the door, making a detour to pick up my raincoat. In the vestibule, a basket filled with feather dusters and rags and tins sat in one corner. The old woman used the force of her entire body to open the door, bending V-shaped with the effort.

The world outside was soggy, tinged a faded yellow. I asked about the tourist office. The old woman shook her head and laughed, stepping over the threshold to join me in the reluctant rain. She put her hand into the large pocket on her left hip and pulled out a pack of cigarettes and a lighter. She offered me a cigarette, but smoking had never agreed with me. Leaning against the doorframe she smoked and waved goodbye. I smiled, pulled up the hood of my jacket and stepped into the faintly drizzly day.

I've lost track of how long I've been in Siramina: the borders between the days are blurred as if seen through a window during a storm. But from that first day, my feet knew where to take me. And it hardly ever seems to rain now, or maybe I've just stopped noticing.

127 Permutations

– Stephanie Reid –

An ordinary street in an ordinary town. In that street, an ordinary house: Number Seventeen. Inside the house; six bedrooms, one lounge, two bathrooms, one kitchen and seven occupants.

The seven occupants, (hereafter referred to individually as persons (A) to (G) and collectively as *the household*) have shared Number Seventeen for two years. Friends/lovers since university, the household interacts smoothly. Minor traumas, upsets or hostilities are tempered by a shared appreciation of world cinema, cabernet sauvignon and Mozart. Efficient access to bathrooms has long since been agreed and the division of domestic responsibilities is now so embedded that the original cleaning rota hangs framed in the lounge – a testament to the stability of living arrangements at Number Seventeen.

These strong foundations support each member of the household. This is how it has always been and how it will continue.

At least for the next three months. Four months from now, <something> will happen causing the household to lose faith in their trinity of wine, world cinema and Wolfgang.

This is how the <something> will occur.

First of all, (A) will stop talking to (B).

This won't be without good reason, but (B) will need a friendly ear and confide in (C).

In support of (B) and because feelings of unease tend to become airborne, (C) will behave more coolly in (A)'s presence.

(D) will sense the animosity and choose not to get involved, although they will state on several occasions that things would be easier for everyone if (A), (B) and (C) could just settle their differences.

Unknown to (B), (A) and (C) will share their disapproval of (D)'s air of superiority. (A) will mimic (D)'s accent one morning, causing (C) to laugh so loudly that (B) will seek out the source of the hilarity.

When (B) enters the kitchen, (C) feeling guilty, will stop laughing.

Will try to make eye-contact with (B) who will refuse.

(A) will then throw their hands in the air and leave.

(C) will sigh and (B) will shake their head in disbelief.

Unlike (D), during this period of unease, (E) and (F) will remain cocooned by the happiness of their four year relationship. This insulation against life's woes will transmit an aura of serenity to their environment and render them largely unaware of any disharmony within Number Seventeen.

In contrast with (E) and (F), (G) will be highly sensitive to this new atmosphere.

Trying to comprehend (E) and (F)'s lack of consciousness about the whole (A)/(B)/(C) situation, (G) will fail and succumb to despair. This will be due in part to (G)'s unfamiliarity with the deep sense of security and elevation the (E)/(F) union affords its members.

(G)'s efforts at understanding will also not be helped by the fact that their own relationship, (which at nine months will be their longest to date) is in demise.

Splitting-up the day before the (A)/(B) difficulties and subsequent (C)/(D) issues arise, (G)'s desire for calm and affection will be understandably heightened.

(G) will begin to unravel; losing both sleep and appetite. They'll also be unable to vocalise the persistent nightmares they're experiencing.

Nightmares they will take as a presentiment of trouble in store for the household.

Unknown to (G), (D) will take note of their unease and call a house meeting.

As (D) will not yet be on speaking terms with (A)/(B)/(C) and (A) will still be having difficulties with (B). The meeting will not go well:

(A) will throw wine over (B).

(C) will accuse (D) of being dictatorial.

(E) and (F) will coerce (G) into discussing their nightmares.

(G) will cry uncontrollably. For over an hour.

In the aftermath of accusations, insults and upsets, the household will reach the conclusion that their differences are irreconcilable and begin dividing up their music and movie collections.

Loud rows concerning the ownership of a particular possession will result in neighbours calling the police.

And arrests.

But for now, all is harmonious within the walls of Number Seventeen. Seven glasses of cabernet sauvignon have been poured for the seven people relaxing on a seven-seater sofa. They watch *Amelie*, laughing as appropriate and blissfully unaware that four months from now, the very same film will lead them to spend a night in their local police station.

Classified

– Joshua Allen –

Thursday, 7th October, 57 years since the birth of the Third Reich (TR 57)

It is best to start with the most urgent matter: the subhuman. He hangs around the library making faces at the books, occasionally sliding one out and underlining the blurb in his drool. They say he was married once, before he was imprisoned for child molestation. He is a dribbler due to the high impurity of crack cocaine, and the high frequency of assaults, in prison. He is called John.

I've decided to start this diary because I feel that the dormant Reich is about to break free again from the insidious fetters of Judaism, Negroism, Communism. It is only I and my Aryan brothers, those who are conscious of their race and its essence as a cosmic superlative, that have kept the legacy of 1933 from being lost entirely to this poisonous amnesia. But who am I? If whoever reads this is a Nietzschean, they will of course be concerned with the *individual*.

I'm a bit of a bookworm myself. From the scuffed purple carpet to the dust on the picture rail, I know the library from cover to cover. It's a Victorian hardback with superficially modern binding. As I stroll through the automatic doors with my rucksack of returns, Alice the librarian makes cursory eye contact, half raises the corners of her mouth and says: 'Morning Matthew.' 'Morning,' I reply. I am filed under M-A-T in her acquaintances department, after Martin the cleaner. Why after? I sometimes want to change my name to 1 1; first in the register, first in Alice's filing cabinet, first in everything. But what if there's someone already called 1 1? Are numbers legally allowed in names? I will research this as soon as possible.

Now in the Reference section, I continue to my seat. You can recognise it by the lack of blackened chewing gum within a two metre radius of its legs; Martin (M-A-R) knows nothing of his alphabetical superiority, thus treats me with undeserved respect. My favourite book is here – *The New Weapons of the World Encyclopaedia: An International Encyclopaedia from 5000 B.C. to the 21st century.* I've touched all 368 pages of this tome, from the flint knives to the M4 assault rifle. I see what they would do to a skull, the exoskeleton with such trembling jewels inside. To tickle the cerebrum while the wretch still feels. To have more power than an adjustable spanner around his scrotum. To hang, draw and quarter him with every ginger probe of a twig in his brain. To communicate in the only way they understand, and to see it played back again and again on the maggot's face as the utter incomprehensibility of suffering dawns on him.

Today I'm reading Friedrich Wilhelm Nietzsche, my bastion of reality in this world of John, Martin and Alice. But what do I know about Alice? She is a woman, whatever that means; she is tall; her skin seems solid; her teeth flash like a lighthouse's lamp. She is a book classification unit. She is a smile maker and an eye maker. She knows who I am in the most perfunctory sense of the term. I doubt she even reads; that is how deep my suspicion of her runs. She has never commented on my repeated renewal of *The New Weapons of the World Encyclopaedia: An International Encyclopaedia from 5000 B.C. to the 21st century.*

Alice is a slave. Alice thinks she does the computer classification and the re-shelving. In fact she *is* the computer classification and the re-shelving. Alice thinks she is paid and then goes home at 5:30pm. In reality she pays herself and is marched home by the invisible death squad to whom time has no meaning. The library controls the air. The library grips the pavement. The library is in her shoes. I've seen her smoking outside the automatic doors and talking on her mobile. Perhaps she has a man; he will be used to the transparent dust on her face now. It's inevitable. I've considered turning her ivory teeth into black notes, flats and sharps, by playing them *allegro* with a hammer.

Martin is a slave. Martin thinks he does the cleaning. Anyone can see that he *is* the cleaner. Martin sees freedom at 6:00pm when he takes off his uniform and combs his arid scalp with grease. All of this is arbitrarily determined by the sulphur gas of the strip lighting. All of this is wood pulp and glue and ink. Martin's last conscious act is retreat into happiness. He once saw me studying the Thompson and MP45 sub-machine guns of *The New Weapons of the World Encyclopaedia: An International Encyclopaedia from 5000 B.C. to the 21st century* and started talking about the film *Saving Private Ryan*. He said, 'The hell those guys had to go through for their country...can you imagine it?' I nodded gravely and made a "Hmmm" noise. Of course those soldiers did not go through anything. To say they died is a tautology; they were always dead. A being fulfilling its essential function is not active, it is its *existence*. I feel that "Hmmm" expressed this in a profound way that he could not possibly understand, for he is a cleaner.

John is not a slave. John is a subhuman. John does not think that he dribbles, but he is a dribbler. John's name is close to 'justice' in the filing system; there is an error here, as justice is in no way responsible for John's name being closer to '1 1' than mine.

Martin picks up John's discarded books and wipes them. Alice has protected the books with plastic sleeves. They are both slaves to a subhuman...

Sunday, 10th October, TR 57

My father finished his tour of the Falklands when I was seven. I imagined him flying low over the ocean, the targeting system of his Sea Harrier hovering over an Argentinian cruiser like a wrathful ghost. He was imperial in his flying helmet and grey suit. He was the cool circuitry in a missile. His hand was steadily guiding the joystick. He moved his thumb over the red-ridged fire button. He pushed. An air-to-ground missile fizzed into the cruiser, annihilating it completely. He was the hammer-headed lightning of Thor. He was the Übermensch.

I haven't spoken to my mother since 1991, when he crashed like a screaming eagle into Iraq. He would have incinerated the hook-nosed scum.

Tuesday, 12th October, TR 57

The UK Deed Poll Office replied to my email. You can change your name to 'Tarquin Fin-tim-lin-bin-whin-bim-lim-bus-stop-F'tang-F'tang-Olé-Biscuitbarrel', as did the Raving Loony candidate in the 1981 Crosby by-election, but the name '1 1' is restricted. They are slaves to the snivelling Jewish *ressentiment* that has usurped our aristocratic culture. The only other option was 'A A'. I'm taking the train to the UK Deed Poll Office tomorrow.

Finally, it'll be official: I will be first. I have always been first. Nietzsche the philologist would understand; 'it's all in a name'. To change a name is to change reality, morality, the totality! Anything is possible.

But today as I enter the library, the inevitable assault of the subhuman has begun; John is holding *The New Weapons of the World Encyclopaedia: An International Encyclopaedia from 5000 B.C. to the 21st century*. I can see a gobbet of drool hanging inches above its cover. This is it – the flashpoint.

I swing my backpack off my shoulder, ramming its payload of books into his jowly throat. He splutters in surprise and clutches the book to his face as a shield. He stumbles back and trips over a low chair, falling hard on his back. His expression is mildly more stultified than usual. He still has the book, and is making a whining noise like a beaten dog. I crack my leather shoe down on his knuckle, and he screams at a pitch exactly proportional to the force of my sole. I grind my foot until his hand loosens, then snatch the book from his grasp. I kick him in the ribs for good measure, then take my seat behind the nearest shelf in the Reference section. Thankfully, the Stalinist nannies have yet to install CCTV cameras inside libraries.

Alice came running with a predictably pursed mouth and wide eyes; I stood up from my seat and assumed a look of concerned disbelief. 'He just collapsed, I think he's getting worse you know.' She opened her mouth and closed it again. 'Help me get him up, Matthew.' I reach down at the same moment as Alice, allowing me to say, 'God, he's scared of *you*, isn't he?' when he screams again. Alice exhales a short sigh, we grab an arm each and dump his vapid form on another chair. John seems to be crying. I walk away.

This is not the first time I've executed some retributive justice on a cretin. Only last month an unshaven tramp asked me for change and I spat on him. I thought the taste of a master's saliva might have a salutary effect. After he tried to grab my leg, I tracked him down at night and bludgeoned his rotting head in with a steel tube. As it was Christmas Eve,

I made a little play with his severed head. He played John the Baptist; I played Octavian, master of the Jews.

Friday, 15th October, TR 57

Today the shelves are alive with the sound of gunfire. The whistling ricochets bounce from every corner of the library, and Alice continues oblivious. She is reordering the computer system in the siege of Stalingrad. A stick grenade explodes metres away. She clicks and types. I stay low, clutching *The New Weapons of the World Encyclopaedia* to my chest like a breastplate. Totally obsolete against a .50 calibre round, but comforting none the less.

The subhuman John has not reappeared in several days. Clearly my official name, A A, has philologically established my absolute supremacy. But I wouldn't expect him to understand that.

Having no degenerate-owned propaganda-box at home, I watch some of the Nuremberg rally on the library computer. Intellectually substandard, but the manifestation of the will to power takes many forms. The ignorant shout 'Nazi!' when I wear my BNP shirt, not knowing that truly Nietzschean parties are expansionist rather than nationalist, and fascist rather than socialist; the National Socialist label was only ever a hook to grab the slaves' votes. Sadly, Hitler couldn't function without the working class after the First World War destroyed the aristocracy. Nowadays, we won't have to build concentration camps, we'll just seal the council estates and pump in the Zyklon B.

As the video finishes and I remove my headphones, there is a strange scratching at the redbrick window. A pigeon is there dressed in a navy blue waistcoat, white breeches and a broad black hat. I realise that it is Napoleon Bonaparte, the only Übermensch in recent history. He is dragging his beak over the glass like a blunt scalpel. It is as if he wants to break the transparent yet impenetrable time that separates us, to thrust his *geist* once more into the fray of strong against weak. I cannot pity him, that foul Christian sentiment, but I quickly smash the glass with my fist, grab his neck and pull him in. He is cooing softly, a slight gurgle and struggling wings. But what is this? As I hold him in my hands, they are warm and wet…there is blood on the window and a gash in his neck. He is dead.

Wednesday, 20th October, TR 57

The broken window was difficult to explain, but not as challenging to their factory-farmed schemata as what appeared to be a slaughtered avian placed lightly on the computer keyboard and left to drip. To the educated eye, the blood on the keys was the sacrifice of classical language to the parasites of liberal media and culture, a metaphor for the dilution of the Aryan race through their negrified trash. To Martin and Alice it was utterly inexplicable. John had never been prone to violence and he never ventured into the IT area…but his sticky scarlet hands were proof enough? Perhaps his collapse the other day was a precursor to this psychotic act? I, needless to say, branded him with the vital fluid before purging myself of it in the sink. The sight of the pathetic cretin being persecuted for his false stigmata, Christ-like in his concealed anger and his aura of naivety, tickled me royally. And finally he was removed from the library, resettled to a place where his kind could not infect the living. At last there was Lebensraum, a place where the ideals of the Reich could be pursued without the parasitic pity that our democracy has internalised in its brainwashed subjects.

My ambiguous attraction to Alice grows stronger now that she has seen John for what he is. As an Aryan and a woman, it will not take her long to be convinced that racial purity and the will to power are the only solutions to our corruption by the inferior. It is the personal duty of every Aryan to procreate, another natural manifestation of the up-going, the overcoming that is inherent to the strong. She has looked at me differently since I "helped" John after the book incident; how ironic that my compassionate façade might accidentally further the Aryan race! Perhaps her cold blue eyes, like the sky from which the Valkyries descend to carry the heroes to Valhalla, could be the compliment to my fiery fury. She could be my Eva.

Friday, 29th October, TR 57

I am in my usual seat, re-reading *Mein Kampf.* A man I have never seen before enters the library, yet there is something familiar about him. Is he the keeper of a shop I once visited? He is wearing a tan mac, grey suit trousers, straight-edged glasses and a brimmed hat. Making a quiet greeting to Alice, he looks briefly in my direction and then exits through the doors. Alice looks over at me and for the first time, she smiles; a broad grin that seems to impart a shared joke. Presuming that she was amused by the man's strange behaviour, I smile back…ah, she is mine! I close the book and walk over to her as nonchalantly as possible, my chest filled with virile exuberance.

'Police! Hands behind your head!' I hear. An armed response unit, MP5's at their shoulders, seems to appear from every corner of the library at once. Standing behind them is the man in the grey mac, a wry smirk wrinkling his cheeks. An involuntary cramp seizes my ribcage; slowly removing his glasses and hat, despite the unglazed eyes and firm jaw, I see the face of John, the subhuman. He was always a subhuman…but now his irises flash with penetrating knowledge. The butt of a gun hits me in the small of the back, paralysing my hips and legs. Gasping, I fall to my knees as they wrench my arms behind my back and snap the handcuffs shut.

A week has passed since my last diary entry, a week of torture and confinement. I secured a copy of this diary after they took the original for evidence. I have been classed a domestic terrorist by the so-called government, allowing them to treat me like a damn Arab; water-boarding, sexual degradation and sensory deprivation, all performed by blacks to add perversion to injury. They tortured me passionately, they tortured me stoically, they tortured me despite my admittance of everything, they tortured me for my lack of remorse, they tortured me for my tears of pain. And always standing behind the niggers was John, only stepping forward once to spit in my face after I shouted 'Subhuman!' at him. He thought a master's saliva would have a salutary effect on a psycho, he quipped.

I couldn't help but laugh, great guffaws bouncing from the lenses of John's glasses, pinging off the walls like bullets, striking the bald greasy head of one of the blacks and spinning a Pythagorean net of luminous angles in that cream concrete cave. Through the laughter, which now seems to be coming from the walls in a screeching crescendo of feedback, I hear him shout, 'You Nazi motherfucker! Don't you know what you've done? Fuck it, we're sending him to D53a.' And that's where I am now, living incognito in a stinking pit full of starving Arabs. There have been ten suicides this month. With no hope of release, no books, and this being my last piece of paper, I have decided to do the same. Nihilism? I am weak and must be punished. The will to power takes many forms. I am only its conduit and it has chosen the strong, as is inherent. It is best that no-one reads this, the weak would only make a martyr of me like that miserable Semite on his cross. The Führer must die, long live the Führer!

Unthologists

Sarah Evans has had dozens of stories published in magazines and competition anthologies over the last five years. *On such a night* was a runner up for Bridport 2008. *His Mother Tongue* won first place in the 2009 Legend Writing Award. *Afterwards* won first place in the Oct 2010 Writers' Forum monthly competition. *The Chose* appears in the 2011 Earlyworks Press anthology. She lives in Welwyn Garden City with her husband.

Lander Hawes is a Norwich based writer. Now in his mid-thirties, most of his working life so far has been part-time in order to allow him to write. His stories have been published online, he has read on the radio and at events, and has had one story accepted by a University of East Anglia journal. Lander is married to the lovely Sarah.

Shanta Everington has an MA in Creative Writing with Distinction from Manchester Metropolitan University and teaches Creative Writing with The Open University. Shanta's debut novel, *Marilyn and Me*, was shortlisted for the Cinnamon Press First Novel Award and published in 2007. *Give Me a Sign*, her first young adult novel, followed in 2008 with Flame Books. *Hang Up* was originally shortlisted for The Bridport Prize in 2009 and has been looking for a home ever since. Other stories appear in anthologies *Even More Tonto Short Stories* and the *Mosaic* anthology with Bridge House Publishing. Her poems have appeared in the *Refuge* anthology, *Envoi* and other small press publications. Shanta is a contributing writer for *The View From Here* literary magazine. More details can be found at www.shantaeverington.co.uk

Melissa Mann's poetry and stories have been published in anthologies and literary magazines worldwide. She has had fiction short-listed and highly commended in the Harpers & Queen/Orange Prize for Fiction short story competition, The Asham Award (twice) and the London Arts New Writing competition. Her poetry book, *baby, i'm ready to go* is out now published by Grievous Jones Press. More details at www.melissamann.com

Ashley Stokes's first novel *Touching the Starfish* was published by Unthank Books in 2010.

Nick Sweeney has collected (and paid) income tax, served drinks, washed glasses, taught English, and edited a million pages of text, most of it not his own. He has published short stories and his first novel *Laikonik Express* was published by Unthank Books in 2011. He lives and works in London as a musician, editor and writer.

Paul A. Green grew up in London, studied at Oxford and University of British Columbia, UBC Creative Writing MA). His poetry and short fiction have appeared in *Angels of Fire, Prism International, Poetry Review, New Worlds*. More recently on-line in: *Great Works, Toxic Poetry, Shadow Train, The Recusant, Nth Position*. His plays include: *The Dream Laboratory* (CBC Radio Canada); *Ritual of the Stifling Air* (BBC Radio); *The Mouthpiece* (Resonance FM); *Power/Play* (Capital Radio); *The Voice Collection* (RTE Ireland); *Terminal Poet* (New Theatre Works) and *Babalon* (Travesty Theatre) based on the life of Crowleyite rocket scientist Jack Parsons. Iain Sinclair describes his novel *The Qliphoth* as "A word quest launched from the edge-lands of arcane knowledge."

Tessa West was awarded the Arthur Welton Award while writing her first biography *The Curious Mr Howard* about the prison reformer John Howard. It was published by Waterside Press in 2011. She has published three novels, *The Estuary, The Reed Flute* and *Companion to Owls*, and a collection of poems entitled *The Other Vikings*. She is now working on another novel. Her short story *Parallax* appeared in *Unthology 1*.

Charles Wilkinson was born in Birmingham and educated at the Universities of Lancaster, East Anglia and Trinity College, Dublin. Iron Press published a collection of his poems in 1987 and *The Pain Tree and Other Stories* appeared from London Magazine Editions in 2000. He has also had fiction in *Best Short Stories 1990* (Heinemann), *Best English Short Stories II* (Norton) and anthologies published by LME and Little, Brown Book Group. Recent poems have been printed in *Poetry Wales, Poetry Salzburg, THE SHOp, Tears in the Fence, The Interpreter's House* and other journals. He divides his time between a flat in Birmingham and his home in Powys.

Ian Madden's short fiction has appeared in the *Edinburgh Review* and several anthologies including the Bridport Prize. In 2010 he was runner-up in the Bristol Short Story Prize and was awarded first prize in *By Invitation Only: A Collection of Short Stories* published to mark National Short Story Week.

M. Pinchuk has lived in Turkey, Thailand, the United Kingdom and the United States. She has studied in Cairo. Her stories have been nominated for a Pushcart Prize and included in anthologies of new writing in the United Kingdom (*New Writing 14*, Granta) and in China. Her work has also appeared in *Lumina* and *Word Riot*, and excerpts from *Architecture*, a collection of short writings about places and spaces, were included in an audio tour of an outdoor sculpture exhibition at the Helen Day Art Center in Stowe, Vermont.

Stephanie Reid is currently completing a joint BA in London and intends to continue exploring the links between Social Science and Literature. She is also developing a novella that she aims to complete in 2012.

Joshua Allen was born in a small village near Tonbridge, Kent, on St. David's Day 1988. While pursuing careers in entomology, art, literature and military technology he attended various educational institutions which taught him to despise himself. Despite these academic setbacks, he opted to continue at the University of East Anglia, where he graduated in English Literature and Philosophy in 2010. Since then, he has quit working at an insurance company and started caring for elderly people with dementia in Norwich, primarily for the more engaging conversation.

Lightning Source UK Ltd.
Milton Keynes UK
UKOW050240041111

181434UK00001B/11/P